WE ESCAPE

by
Judit Makranczy

Judit Makranczy
May 1999

Royal Fireworks Press
Unionville, New York

Dedication

To my mother, Justine Maday for her incredible courage, convictions and love. To my family, Andrea, Attila, Aniko, Alexa and Vanessa. To Susan Gin, for her encouragement and support. To Ryan Johnson, for his thoughtful critique.

Royal Fireworks Press
First Avenue, PO Box 399
Unionville, NY 10988-0399
(914) 726-4444
FAX (914) 726-3824

ISBN: 0-88092-373-3

Printed in the United States of America on acid-free, recycled paper using vegetable-based inks by the Royal Fireworks Printing Company of Unionville, New York.

Table of Contents

INTRODUCTION

András raced after the tall, lanky boy, intercepted him, and stole the ball in one swift move. Quickly scanning the field, he turned sharply and ran hard toward the goal. Dribbling past two defenders, András looked at the goalkeeper, faked to the right, and kicked the soccer ball hard into the upper left corner of the net. *Goal!* András smiled as he trotted to the sidelines. He was drenched with sweat, his light brown hair plastered to his high forehead.

"Good play, András!" Coach Edwards said, slapping him on the back as András grabbed a towel to wipe his face. Someone jabbed him hard in the side. András yanked the towel away from his face and spun around.

"Why didn't you pass the ball to Mike? He could have made the goal!" Brad yelled at András.

"Mike too far," András replied, standing his ground.

Brad imitated András, "'Mike too far!' You sound like a stupid caveman."

"Yeah, a stupid foreign caveman," Jason butted in. "Give it up! You're never gonna be an American, András. That stupid accent of yours is a dead give-away."

"Little Attila the Hun thinks he can do it all by himself! You should have passed the ball to me!" Mike pointed an angry finger in András's face.

Brad stared at András, his eyes filled with rage. "We've told you before, quit hogging the ball, or you'll be sorry!" Brad turned his back toward András, lifted his right arm to scratch his head then suddenly swung it back, his elbow slamming into András' ribs. András doubled over, clutching his side. Brad quickly glanced over his shoulder at him. A small smile of satisfaction spread across his lips as he walked away.

András felt hot tears roll down his face. He straightened up painfully, wiping the tears away with the towel. Maybe he should have passed the ball to Mike. They were up by one goal. But he knew Mike couldn't have scored, and being up by two goals guaranteed his team a win in the final minutes of the game.

"Hey, are you okay?" Coach Edwards asked, walking up to him. "Bad side-stitch, eh András. Well, it'll pass."

The game was over. Coach Edwards joined the rest of the team, congratulating them on the win. The other boys didn't even look at András. When he first joined the city league, the boys, all freshmen in high school, kidded András about being in sixth grade and praised his skills on the field. Now, halfway through the season, they hated him. He held the team record in goals and steals.

As the team began to walk toward the parking lot, Brad, Jason and Mike hung back. András watched them. He didn't want to get beaten up again. He desperately wanted them to understand how much soccer meant to him, that it was the one thing he could excel at, the one thing he could do and not feel like an outsider. András cursed quietly in Hungarian. The three boys walked over and surrounded him. Brad, who was behind András, suddenly grabbed his shorts, and yanked them down. The boys laughed as András scrambled to pull his pants up. Quickly tucking his shirt in, András glanced up and saw Brad's younger sister, Jennifer, staring at him. They were in the same sixth grade class. András felt the sudden flush of heat burning his face. Turning abruptly, he grabbed his sports bag, jumped on his bicycle and peddled furiously across the street.

Speeding through the small shopping center toward his neighborhood, his thoughts bounced between the humiliation he'd just experienced and the knowing satisfaction of having played an excellent game. He understood the jealousy of his teammates but not their cruel behavior. Pumping hard, he jumped the curb with his bike and sailed past honking cars.

Turning left on Norton Avenue, András suddenly stopped. He couldn't go home, not yet. It was impossible to hide his anger and hurt from his parents. He needed time to calm down.

Slamming his fist on the handlebar, András turned his bike around and headed toward the neighborhood park two blocks away.

Arriving at the small park, he was relieved to see very few children there, all of them toddlers playing in the sandbox.

Throwing his bicycle down on the grass, András wiped hot tears of anger from his eyes and climbed the large old oak tree, quickly reaching the tree house which had been built years ago. He settled back into a corner, feeling invisible.

"Hi," a young voice called to him.

Startled by the sudden, unexpected voice, András jumped up and leaned over the railing. His hands tightened on the worn wood until his fingers hurt. "No! Stay down!" he yelled.

Jennifer stopped climbing up the make-shift ladder that was hammered into the tree and gazed up at him. "I wanted to apologize for my stupid brother," she said firmly, not backing down.

"Yes, Brad stupid. He angry and I angry. Go away." András knew his English was incorrect. The shock of Jenny's presence made him forget to think his sentences through before speaking.

"I won't go away," Jennifer replied and began climbing again. "They're just jealous of you and act like immature jerks because you're so much better at soccer than they are."

Jenny reached the top of the ladder and stepped into the tree house. She leaned against the rail. András had backed away into the farthest corner.

"Look," Jenny began hesitantly, "Brad does stupid things like that to a lot of people."

András looked down at his worn tennis shoes, "Please go," he whispered.

"No." Jenny responded immediately and sat down at the top of the ladder. "You have to fight back, or they'll just keep beating you up and teasing you."

András jerked his head up, "How? What can I do? I win game, and they get mad!" His voice grew tight. "Everytime I score, they want hit me."

"Well..." Jenny rubbed her cheek. "Talk to Coach Edward or...or have your parents talk to my parents. My mom and dad don't know half the bad things Brad..."

"No...no." András answered before Jenny finished her sentence. "My parents no need..." He stopped and took a breath, "....My parents do not need.... I must do this alone."

4

András paused. His eyes grew determined, and he set his jaw. "I was in prison, I was shot at...I will not let Brad stop me from playing soccer!" He finished with a strong and confident voice.

Jennifer's mouth hung open. "You've been shot at and...and in prison?" she asked with disbelief.

András ran his fingers through his hair and shrugged. "It was before we came to America."

"But I thought you flew to the States," Jenny said, looking at him curiously.

"Yes, but we had to escape from Hungary first," András stated matter-of-factly.

"Escape?" asked a surprised Jenny.

András sighed. When he started school, all he said to classmates and teachers was that he was from Budapest, Hungary. He'd kept the details of his family's escape to himself. Looking at Jenny, he noticed her large, soft brown eyes. She was waiting intently for an answer. Gazing at the playground below, András replied, "You cannot understand."

"András Máday, don't you tell me what I can and can't understand! Tell me how you escaped!" Jennifer scolded.

Taken aback by her direct and harsh tone, András began to stutter, "It's not, not important...you...you no understand... I mean you not..." Flustered, András stood quickly, then realized that Jennifer was sitting directly in front of the ladder. He shrugged sheepishly as Jennifer threw her arms out, further blocking his exit.

"András! You're not leaving here until you've told me about how you escaped and who shot at you and why you were in prison!" she insisted.

"Okay, okay." He shrugged and smiled shyly at her. The soft breeze blowing through the thick branches of the tree gently lifted Jenny's ash-blond hair off of her forehead. Conscious of András looking at her, Jenny quickly tucked her hair behind her ears.

"Please, András, I really want to know how you escaped."

He sat down across from her and leaned against the tree house. "It's a long story. My...the English is very hard for me."

"That's okay. I have time," Jenny responded eagerly. "And you're doing just fine. I can understand you perfectly."

Struggling inwardly to translate his vivid memories from Hungarian into English for Jenny, András felt nervous but also excited to share his past. He scratched his arm. "It started with the arrest of Father and Mother. That happened four years before we escaped."

Jenny nodded, her eyes fixed on his face.

CHAPTER ONE

ARRESTED BY THE SECRET POLICE

It was after midnight on November 7th, 1952. I could hear Grandpa snoring through the thick, double doors between our rooms. My older sister, Andrea, slept soundly on the cot. The sofa was my bed. Sinking into the soft cushions every night, I imagined I was entering another world, invisible to everyone in the room.

Mom and Dad were curled up on the old metal bed. I stared at Mother's stomach for a long time. She was pregnant with twins. Her belly was huge. Mom said the twins would be born in early February. Three more months, and she already had difficulty tying her shoes because she couldn't bend over easily. I wasn't sure how I felt about having babies around the house, especially two! I knew that the chances of having a little brother were a lot better with twins. Maybe both of them would be boys! I decided I'd make them call me "Sir András the Powerful." After all, I would be almost eight years old in February.

I closed my eyes and started drifting off to sleep when I heard a loud knock on the door of our apartment. Dad immediately sat up in bed. I pulled the covers over my head, peeking out from beneath my blanket just enough to see most of the room. Dad stood and put his robe on. Mom sat up awkwardly and grabbed his arm. Even in the dark I could see she was scared.

"Kálmán, what is it?" she asked him quietly.

"I don't know," he replied, moving hesitantly toward the door.

There was a second knock, longer and more insistent. Dad opened the door into the entry and closed it quietly behind him.

I heard the heavy wooden door of our apartment creak open and a strong, deep voice ask, "Are you Kálmán Máday?"

Dad answered, "Yes."

"Get dressed. You're coming with us."

I looked at Mother. She had her robe on and stood frozen in the middle of the dark room. Her eyes were fixed on the closed door. She reached down to turn on the bedside lamp just as Dad opened the door and stepped in. Behind him were two men. Neither of them wore a uniform. One of them wore a heavy gray overcoat and a black suit with a white shirt under it. The other man wore a thick green sweater under his coat and dark brown pants. Both men had wide belts around their waists. That's when I noticed the guns. Each man had a black holster attached to his belt. My eyes darted back to the collars on their overcoats. Squinting hard, I focused on the stripes sewn on their collars. They were red! I bit hard on the corner of my pillow to keep from crying out. They were members of the secret police!

Mom had talked to Andrea and me about them before. She explained that the regular police wore gray uniforms with dark green trim around the collar and cuffs of their coats. The visor of their caps was also dark green. She pointed out the stripes on their collars telling us that the different colors signified their rank.

8

Mom said many members of the secret police wore regular clothes like ordinary people, "That's part of the reason they call them 'secret.' You can't tell they're policeman just by their clothes." She said there was one way we could always tell who was a member of the secret police, by the color of the insignia they wore on their collars: Blood red.

One day as we walked home from the grocery store, I remember asking Mother, "What's so bad about them?"

"It's what they do," she replied, then added, "Don't ever talk to them. They may stop you on the way home from school and ask you about your father or grandfather."

"Ask me what?"

"Things like where they work or who their friends are." Then Mom stopped suddenly and in the voice she uses when I know I'm in trouble, she said, "If the secret police or anybody, and I mean anybody, ever asks you if somebody is a friend of your father's, tell them you don't know."

I nodded my head slowly but immediately thought of Uncle László, Mom's older brother who came to visit us often and was one of Dad's best friends. "But if a secret policeman asks me if Dad knows Uncle László, what am I supposed to say?"

Mom shook her head. I could tell she was frustrated by the look on her face. "Just tell them your mother told you not to talk to strangers. You can tell them that. I told you that before anyway."

But I still wanted to know who these men were. "Mom, what do the secret police do?"

She didn't say anything. I thought she wasn't going to answer my question or couldn't answer it, and then she responded, "They can do anything they want to, and they don't have to tell you why. You know Mr. and Mrs. Tóllas in apartment 122 downstairs? Last week the secret police arrested both of them. Nobody knows where they are. Mrs. Tóllas's sister, Éva, has been to every police station in the city begging for information. No one will tell her anything."

I stared at Mother. I liked Mr. and Mrs. Tóllas. They were about the same age as Mom and Dad, in their early 30's, but they didn't have any children.

"Why did they arrest them?"

Mom's face was drawn and tight. I knew she didn't want to talk about it, but I just had to know. Maybe they robbed a bank or murdered somebody and chopped him up!

She took a deep breath and was about to answer when a small, loud group of factory workers came up from behind and passed us on the sidewalk. She waited until they crossed the street and were well ahead of us before she said in a quiet voice, "Mr. and Mrs. Tóllas were listening to foreign broadcasts on their radio."

"Oh." But I really didn't understand and was very disappointed they hadn't done something really terrible. *What was bad about listening to the radio?* I figured I could get away with asking one more question before Mom told me to stop being so curious.

"How did the secret police know they were listening to foreign broadcasts?"

Mom gave me a sharp look, then in a louder voice replied, "Someone turned them in."

"You mean someone told the secret police?"

"Yes."

She didn't even look at me when I asked, "Who?" I knew she was wondering if she should say anything else to me.

Shifting the sack of groceries in her arms, Mom turned her head to look behind us and then firmly said, "Someone in our apartment building."

There was a spy in our building! This was almost as good as the Tóllas's being bank robbers! I couldn't wait to get home and tell my friend, Péter, who was 14 and lived one floor above us. Maybe he could help me find the spy!

I stared at the men standing in our room. *What did they want from my father? We didn't listen to foreign broadcasts on the radio.* The older man ordered Dad to get dressed. Father moved to the chair where his clothes were neatly folded and quickly put them on. He was tall and slender. His wavy, dark brown hair, which he combed straight back, fell into his green eyes as he bent to pull on his socks. Mom always said he was the most handsome huszár soldier she'd ever met. They married near the end of World War II. Dad wouldn't tell me much about the war except that the huszár divisions were the best trained soldiers in all of Hungary. After the war, Dad went to work as a customs agent for the national railroad. Mom told Andrea and me that the government controlled everything,

11

all of the schools, the stores, transportation, the newspapers, and where people could work.

Father glanced at Mom as he pulled his shoes on. Mom didn't move. She just stared at him. The two men stood like statues.

I wanted to jump out of bed and demand to know what the secret police wanted with my father. I wanted to tell them to leave, that they were making a mistake. Most of all, I wanted to demand the name of the spy who told them about Dad.

The younger policeman looked over at me and took a step in my direction. I squeezed my eyes shut and tried not to breath. The older man told Dad to hurry up.

I opened my eyes and peered from under the warm blanket. Father finished dressing and walked over to Mom. He put both of his strong hands on her shoulders and looked into her eyes. Neither of them said a word. The older secret policeman stepped forward, grabbed Dad by the arm and said, "Let's go." They left quietly, closing the door behind them.

Mom just stood there. I wanted to let her know I was awake, but I felt paralyzed. I couldn't move. I couldn't speak. I couldn't even think.

Mom looked over at Andrea, then at me before walking silently to the door leading to Grandfather's room. I saw the light come on under the door and heard Grandfather's voice. I didn't understand why Father was taken away, and why in the middle of the night? I strained to hear what they were saying in the next room, but the voices were so low, I couldn't hear clearly. I dropped my head on the pillow, feeling defeated. Closing my eyes, I willed myself

12

to stay awake and was surprised when I heard Mom telling me to get up and get ready for school. She didn't say anything else as she headed back to the kitchen. It was 6:30 a.m. I dragged myself off of the sofa and started folding the blankets and sheets. I noticed Andrea's cot was already made. She was probably in the kitchen with Mom. I was tired and frightened, more frightened than I had ever been in my life. At least that's what I thought until three days later.

CHAPTER TWO

A SPY IN THE BUILDING

Three days after Dad was taken away, my teachers found out about it. First thing that morning, Mrs. Maxa made me stand at my desk and announced that my father was an enemy of the State; an enemy of the Communist Party.

I was so mad and embarrassed, I yelled at her, "My father is not an enemy, you're lying! You're lying!"

Mrs. Maxa's face began turning purple. She rushed over to me and almost pulled my arm out of its socket as she dragged me out of the classroom.

She pulled my face right up to hers and told me in a furious voice, "Your father was arrested because he was protecting a friend of his who was printing an illegal newspaper."

"What's wrong with printing a newspaper?" I asked defiantly.

"He was printing lies about the government, lies about our leaders, and lies about the Soviet Union!" she spit back at me. "This man is our enemy, and your father helped him hide from the police. That makes your father an enemy too!"

I thought I was going to faint, not only because of what she said, but because her breath was terrible. Our faces were just inches apart. I tried to wriggle free of her tight grip, but she'd practically lifted me off of the floor.

Mrs. Maxa finally let go of my arm, and I dropped my head to take a deep breath.

"Never talk to me like that again! Do you understand?"

I nodded but didn't look at her. She propelled me back into the classroom. All my classmates stared as I quickly sat down.

I didn't move or say a word the rest of the day. When the final bell rang, I ran out of the building as fast as I could, not bothering to take my book bag. Andrea finally caught up with me halfway home. She began yelling at me because I didn't have my books. I told her to shut up and ran the rest of the way to our apartment.

Mom and Grandfather weren't home when I walked in the door. I knew Andrea would be home soon and I didn't want to see her so I ran out, down the hall and up one flight of stairs to Péter's apartment. I sat in the hallway until I heard him coming up the stairs. I jumped up and met him on the landing.

"I heard what happened in school today," he said quietly and tousled my hair.

I looked up at him and asked, "Remember when I told you there was a spy in our building?"

Péter shook his head. He'd told me it was true, but he wouldn't help me find out who it was. He just said I was wasting my time and not to bother.

"Well, I think it was the spy who told the secret police about my dad."

Péter sat down on the top stair and leaned against the stained, white wall.

"I've got to find out who he is, Péter!"

15

He turned to look up at me. "And what are you going to do when you find this spy?"

"I'll turn him in to the police and then they'll let Dad go!" I replied.

Péter stared at me. "That's the stupidest thing I ever heard. Use your head, moron! The spy is working for the secret police. And how do you know it's a male? It could be a female."

"A woman spy?" I couldn't believe it.

Péter reached over and gently punched me on the chin. "Shut your mouth before something unpleasant flies into it." He stood up and started walking toward his apartment. Reaching the door, Péter turned and quietly said, "I'm sorry about your father."

I started slowly down the stairs to my apartment. And then it dawned on me. I knew who the spy was! I rushed down the steps two at a time and burst into our apartment. Andrea was doing her homework at the kitchen table.

"I know who turned Dad in!" I blurted.

She dropped her pen and looked at me with serious eyes. "You can't know. Even Mother doesn't know!"

"But I do know," I insisted.

"Okay smartie, who is it?" she asked.

"Mrs. Nagy." I answered triumphantly.

Andrea rolled her eyes and picked up her pen. "She's been living here for seven years. Besides, she's old and minds her own business."

"Yes, but Péter said the spy could be a woman, and since she lives with us, she knows all of Dad's friends and

Mrs. Maxa said Dad was hiding a friend of his. That's why he got arrested."

Andrea looked at me as if she were going to kill me.

"Don't you ever talk about this again. You don't know who told on Dad, and it wasn't Mrs. Nagy!" '

But I just knew it had to be her. Mom told me that seven years ago some officials from City Hall came to talk to Grandfather. They told him that, according to the new housing laws, he had too much living space for one person. He didn't need three rooms. They said he could keep two of the rooms because he was a doctor. However, they were moving someone into the third room. The next day Mrs. Nagy moved into Grandfather's apartment.

She was a food manager in one of the more popular restaurants in Budapest. Grandfather had to share his kitchen and the one bathroom with a total stranger!

Three months ago the four of us, Mom, Dad, Andrea and I moved in. Since Grandfather used the smallest room as his bedroom and the other as his office, we moved into the livingroom. The room was large, with three huge windows and a tall ceiling.

Mother and Grandfather came home after dark. Both of them looked very tired. Mom hung up her coat and immediately went into the kitchen to start dinner. Grandfather quietly went to his office and shut the door.

"Any word about Dad?" Andrea asked expectantly. We were sitting at the kitchen table.

Mom finished filling the pot with water and set it on the stove. "No," she said absently.

I was about to tell Mother about Mrs. Maxa and what happened at school when Andrea kicked me hard. I almost yelled out loud, but the look she gave me stopped the scream in my throat.

We ate dinner in silence, and after Andrea and I washed the dishes, Mother, as she did every night, asked to see our homework. Andrea stuck her tongue out at me as she handed her homework to Mom. I knew I was going to be punished for not bringing my books home. When Mother asked me for my homework, I told her I had forgotten my books. She just nodded and told me to get ready for bed. I fell asleep quickly, totally unaware of the terror I would experience just a few hours later.

CHAPTER THREE

THE INTERROGATION

I woke up to unfamiliar voices coming from the entryway of our apartment. Bolting upright in bed, I rubbed my eyes and looked at the clock, 12:30 a.m. Mom was sitting on the edge of her bed. Andrea was still asleep in her cot. Not even an earthquake could wake her once her head sank into the pillow.

I could hear Grandfather's soft, kind voice. He said something about coffee but was interrupted by a strong male voice.

"Justine Máday."

I jerked my head toward Mom.

Grandfather quietly opened the door to our dark room, took a few steps in and, without turning on the lights, simply said, "There are two men who wish to talk to you." A few strands of his long, silver hair hung in his face.

"All right, I'll get dressed," Mother quietly replied.

I could barely see the two strangers through the half-opened door. Both men were young. One had a friendly, oval face with a bushy, light-brown mustache. The second man was tall and thin. His nose was long and bent with a pronounced bump in the middle. Both had blood red stripes on their coat collars.

Grandfather stepped back into the entry and quietly closed the door.

Mother struggled to her feet and started dressing in the dark. She glanced toward Andrea and me a couple of times,

19

but didn't say a word. I just stared at her. She seemed so calm! I started to tell her not to go, but she quietly told me to go back to sleep. "But Mom, you can't..." I began in protest.

"Shhh, I have to go."

I knew there was nothing I could say to stop what was happening. My mind felt like exploding. I wanted to rush into the entry and order the secret police to leave. I saw myself pushing them out the door, yelling at them that they had no right to take my mother. I wanted to demand they bring my father back. I wanted so much to change what was happening! But I didn't move; I couldn't move. I felt totally helpless hiding under the blanket.

I heard the men talking with Grandfather. One of them asked Grandpa what he did for a living, and Grandfather, in his calm voice, told them he was a doctor, a psychiatrist and had his office here in the apartment. He explained that he had worked with Freud and Adler in Vienna many years ago. The tone of the men changed as they asked him questions about the famous Viennese psychiatrists. These men sounded so nice! I imagined they were patients of Granddad's, here to talk about their problems. Any minute now, they would thank Grandpa for his help and leave quietly.

Mother finished dressing and stepped into the entry without closing the door. I saw the look of shock on their faces as they stared at her large stomach. The young man with the mustache looked scared. He asked her, "How far along are you?"

"I'm nine months pregnant," she replied matter-of-factly, although she was really only six-and-a-half months pregnant. But she did look very big because she was expecting twins.

The mustached man took a deep breath and told her to come with them. They left quickly, and Grandfather quietly closed the door to our room.

I jumped out of bed, jerked the door open to the entry and looked at Grandfather. He glanced down at me in surprise. Putting his hand on my shoulder, we stood there in silence for a moment, and then he turned toward the kitchen.

"Go put your robe on, and I'll make some hot chocolate for us."

I walked back into our dark room. Andrea was still asleep. I looked at her and thought of waking her up, but it didn't seem important. Nothing seemed important anymore. My mind was numb and empty. I put my robe on, gazed at my parents' unmade bed and shuffled over to it. I slowly pulled the sheets and covers over the pillows and smoothed out the wrinkles.

When I stepped into the kitchen the kettle was just beginning to whistle. Grandpa motioned for me to sit and poured the hot water into our cups. We didn't say a word. He looked so tired. Mom was the youngest of his three children. Uncle Béla, Mom's oldest brother, left Hungary with his family at the end of the World War II. He lived in America, in California. I had never seen him. Her second brother, Uncle László, lived with his wife on the other side of the city, across the Danube river in Buda. He was an engineer for a company that made big farm equipment, and his wife worked in a flower shop. They came to visit us every week, and Uncle László would tell

21

the most outrageous stories to Andrea and me. He had a soft voice, and his movements were so fluid! He was a lot like Grandpa and seeing the two of them together was like watching a graceful ballet.

Grandfather looked at me for a long time. His face was soft and kind, his eyes a transparent gray. He put his hand on mine, and I grabbed it, afraid he would pull it away, afraid he would send me to bed. I just couldn't go back to the room. Grandpa smiled gently and nodded his head.

I awoke to the lights being turned on in our room, and several voices talking in low tones. Grandfather must have carried me back to bed. Mother was home! I almost jumped up when I saw her but froze when I saw that the two men who had taken her away were standing in the doorway. My heart stopped for an instant and then began beating so fast I thought I was going to die.

I quickly glanced at the clock. It was 4:30 a.m. Pretending to sleep, I forced myself to breath deeply through my nose. I heard Mom tell the men that this was the only room she had in the apartment.

I barely opened my eyes to peek at Mother. She looked exhausted but calm. The two men seemed more relaxed than before as they stepped into the room and began looking around. They were searching for something but it didn't seem very important to them because their movements were very casual, as if they were looking for a pair of lost glasses that they didn't really need. I stole a glance at Andrea and was surprised that she was awake. Neither of us moved as our eyes locked for a brief instant.

The man with the mustache was at Mother's bed, lifting the mattress, pillows and covers. The other secret

22

policeman opened the small box Mom kept on the antique nightstand next to her bed. He held up the English dictionary he'd found and looked at Mom.

"So, you're learning English, are you?"

"Yes," Mom calmly replied.

The man stared at Mom, expecting her to say more. She didn't.

He smiled slightly, then turned his attention back to the box. Mom walked over to Andrea and started speaking quietly, telling her to go back to sleep. She quickly glanced at the men who looked a little embarrassed about waking us up. As Mother came over to me and began gently rubbing my back, telling me to go to sleep, the man who had found the dictionary was looking at the white crocheted cloth covering the nightstand. His back was toward us. I felt Mom's entire body go rigid but her voice was calm as she continued talking to me. Her eyes were fixed on the man's back. I stared in his direction, and held my breath. The beak-nosed man lifted the corner of the cloth draped over the front of the nightstand. There was no drawer. He moved on to the tall closet in the corner of the room which his partner was already searching.

But there was a drawer in that small nightstand, not in the front or the back but on the side! What Mother had hidden in that drawer was strictly forbidden by the government. They could take her away again—only this time, she wouldn't return for years!

The day after my father was taken away, one of his friends from the customs office came by the apartment. Standing in the entryway, he explained to Mom that Father had loaned him some money a few weeks ago, and he wanted to pay it back. The man was very nervous and wouldn't accept Mother's invitation to come in. He clutched his cap in his hands, and his eyes shifted constantly. He jammed his fist deep inside of his jacket and pulled out American money. Twenty dollars! He pushed the money into Mother's hands and left immediately. Mom just stared at the bills. She quickly closed the front door and looked at Andrea and me. I could tell from her face that she wished we hadn't been there, wished we hadn't seen the money. She bent down and quickly whispered that the three of us now had a very important secret. She made us promise to keep the secret forever and told us firmly that we must never, no matter who asked us, say anything about the dollars she had just received. Not even to Grandpa or Uncle László. Mom quietly explained that having foreign money, especially American dollars, was absolutely forbidden. Andrea and I solemnly promised not to say a word although neither of us really understood why this was such a big deal. I was however, very proud of the fact that I now had an important secret to hide. Mother stood up and told us to wait in the entryway as she walked into our room. I tip-toed over to the half-opened door and watched her hide the money in the drawer of her nightstand.

The two secret policemen finished searching the closet. There wasn't much else in the room. Andrea had a suitcase under the cot, well hidden by the blankets which reached the floor. Neither of the men approached her.

Mom stood up from the sofa and calmly asked, " Is there anything else?"

"No," the beak-nosed man replied.

Grandfather, still dressed in his suit, stood quietly by the door. The two strangers said "Goodbye, doctor," as they stepped into the entry and walked out the door.

Grandfather came into our room and put his arms around Mother. Both of them looked over at Andrea who was still as a statue. I quickly struggled into my robe and hurried over to them. Andrea moved slowly, wrapping her blanket around her shoulders and following us out to the kitchen. Grandfather put water in the kettle and joined us at the table. Mother closed her eyes for a moment then said, "I saw Kálmán tonight."

CHAPTER FOUR

A TERRIFYING NIGHT

Mother didn't say anything else for a while. She looked at Andrea, then at me. Her face was drained and tight.

"What I'm going to tell you two," she began in a tired voice, "must never be repeated. Both of you are too young to understand everything that's happened, but what you've seen the past three days...well, I can't pretend it didn't take place."

Mother sighed, and then she smiled. Her smile was so wonderful! Andrea looked directly at Mom and in her most serious tone said, "I understand, Mom. We're in trouble and shouldn't talk to anybody about it."

I rolled my eyes at her. She was always trying to act like an adult and make-believe she understood everything they said.

Mom nodded her head. "You've always known."

A look passed between them that made me feel totally left out. I figured it had to be a mother-daughter thing because I didn't understand it, but I knew in that instant that Andrea had just been admitted into the world of adults.

Grandfather broke the silence, "Justine, what did they want?"

Mother pushed her chair back a little to allow more room for her large stomach.

"They took me to the police station at the 7th District. Ágnes, Phil Szász and Kálmán's mother, Margít, were also brought in."

Ágnes was one of my mother's best friends. She was a school teacher. Phil was Dad's third cousin and a close friend.

"We were taken to a small room near the back of the station. It smelled terrible...like vomit. Grandma Margít was so terrified, I thought she was going to faint. Ágnes and I sat her between us on the bench. Phil sat in a chair and wouldn't look at anybody. There were two armed guards in the room with us. We weren't allowed to talk to each other, but Ágnes did manage to whisper to me that they had searched her apartment before bringing her to the station.

"They took Grandma Margít away first. They didn't keep her very long, about twenty minutes. When they brought her back to the room, she turned to the guard and demanded that they take her home immediately. I couldn't believe the way she talked to them! But that grand lady voice of hers surprised them, and they agreed to drive her home at once." Mom shook her head with a slight smile. Grandmother Margít had a way of making people do exactly what she wanted them to do.

"They took Phil next but never brought him back to the room. I think he's been arrested." Mom paused.

I opened my mouth to urge mother to hurry up and tell us what happened to her. Grandfather must have noticed my eagerness because he reached across the table and patted my hand. I swallowed and bit my lower lip.

"I think an hour must have passed before they came for Ágnes." Mom finally continued. "She was so frightened... both of us were. They finally brought her back about thirty minutes later and told her to sit down. Then a guard opened the door and told me to come with him. They escorted me into an office that was pitch black except for a small lamp on a desk at the far end of the room. All I could see was the desk and the three chairs around it. I couldn't tell if there was anything or anyone else in the room because it was so dark. The officer sitting behind the desk told me to sit down. That's when I noticed that there was someone standing behind him but I couldn't see who it was. All I could see were the black pant legs and highly polished black boots. The rest of him was hidden in the shadows. The man sitting at the desk wore black. When I saw the red and blue stripes on his collar I..."

Mother stopped abruptly and turned to Andrea and me. "This man's job is to interrogate and punish people the secret police arrest. Those red and blue stripes on his collar...they're the worst, the cruelest of them all."

Mom closed her eyes for a moment then turned to Grandfather. "He was fat and had a very harsh voice. He started by asking me, 'Where's the gold, the dollars?'"

"I replied, 'What gold, what dollars?'"

"'Don't tell me you've never seen gold or American dollars?' he demanded."

"I told him, 'Of course I have, in 1947, before August 1st.'"

Mother explained that a law had been passed in 1947. This law stated that no later than August 1st, all citizens who had more than three ounces of gold or any foreign currency had to turn it in to the police. No one was allowed to have gold or foreign money for any reason.

She continued. "He insisted on knowing where Kálmán and I had hidden the dollars. I kept telling him we didn't have any."

Mother looked straight at me and quietly said, "I had to lie to protect all of you."

I slowly nodded my head. She'd always told me to be truthful, but I understood, perhaps more clearly than she thought, what she'd just said.

Mother continued in a slow, measured voice. "That filthy man picked up a sheet of paper and started reading off a list of names. The first name was Phil Szász. He asked me what my relationship was with Phil, how I had met him, what I knew about his work and his family. Everything! He asked the same questions about twelve or thirteen people...all family and friends of ours. He even asked me about Béla in America. Of course, he asked me about Emil."

Emil, was the man Dad was accused of hiding from the secret police.

Mom shrugged her shoulders. "I said as little as possible, and this made him very angry. He slammed his fist on the desk and demanded, 'Are you always this calm or are you just pretending to be calm?'"

"I didn't know what to say and without really thinking, I replied, 'What's the difference to you?'"

"'Don't think your pregnancy is going to save you!' he shouted."

"I told him I didn't think it would. That's when I heard the door open behind me. I turned my head and saw Kálmán."

29

Mom smiled slightly. "He said, 'Hello Justine.' I said, 'Hello Kálmán.'"

"I think they wanted to scare me by bringing him in. They probably thought I would give them the information they wanted if I saw that they had my husband. I knew it didn't make any difference whether or not I was scared. I was scared! But they weren't going to let Kálmán go no matter what I said...even if I had told them about the dollars. I really don't know exactly what they wanted to hear from me. If I had told them about the American money, they probably would have kept me much longer, but I think they wanted something more, something that would help prove that Kálmán was guilty of a crime."

Mom looked directly at Andrea and me. "A couple of minutes after the guards brought your dad into the room, they turned and took him out. We hadn't said anything else to each other."

"They kept me there, asking questions and threatening me for another thirty minutes or so. Then, for the first time, I heard the man standing in the shadows behind the desk speak, 'That's enough. Take her away.' I thought they were going to lock me up, but instead, they took me back to the waiting room. Ten minutes later the two men who searched our room came in and brought me back here." She stopped.

No one said a word.

I thought it was incredible! Mother interrogated by a high ranking officer in the Secret Police. I was so proud of her!

Andrea interrupted my thoughts by asking, "But what did they want?"

Mother shook her head, "I don't really know. Other than the money, which they don't know we have, most of the questions were about family members and friends of ours. But they probably already knew the answers. I'm not sure what they wanted to hear."

Grandfather quietly asked, "How long do you think they'll keep Kálmán?"

Mother's eyes welled up with tears.

"I don't know, Dad. I don't even know if they'll keep him in the city. He might be sent to a labor camp somewhere."

"A labor camp?" I blurted out.

"There's no telling what they're going to do with him or where they'll send him. I just pray he doesn't end up in Siberia."

"Siberia!" I shouted. "They can't send him there. It's not fair! He hasn't done anything wrong. It's all Emil's fault. They should send him to Siberia!"

Mother gave me a sharp look.

"There's something you had better accept, young man, even if you don't understand it. Your father has been arrested. The reason for his arrest doesn't have to make sense to you or me or anyone else. We don't know what's going to happen to your father, and there's nothing we can do about it."

Suddenly the events of the past three days felt like a ton of bricks on my chest. I could barely breathe! All at once, I realized what it meant for Mother to be taken away in the middle of the night and interrogated and that I might never see my father again. I tried to stop the lump that

31

was forming in my throat. It grew so rapidly it hurt. I burst into tears and buried my face in my hands. Mother pulled me to her and held me as I sobbed.

"It's almost six," Grandfather said with surprise, "perhaps all of us should try to get some sleep."

"Yes," Mother replied, then turned to me, "You and Andrea can stay home today. I'll write a note for school."

I nodded my head and felt Mother gently push me away from her. She stood up with difficulty and with her arms around Andrea and me, walked us back to our room and tucked us in.

I was exhausted. Pulling the blanket over my head, I fell asleep immediately. I dreamed Mother was being interrogated. Then suddenly the picture changed, and I was the one sitting across from the desk in the dark room. The fat man was leaning toward me and shouting questions so rapidly that I didn't have a chance to respond. I kept opening my mouth to speak, but he wouldn't let me answer him. Then the man standing behind him stepped forward. I couldn't see his face, only the stark black uniform and the pistol in his hand pointed directly at me.

CHAPTER FIVE

THE SEARCH FOR FATHER

The twins were born early, a month and a half before they were due. Grandfather added their names and date of birth to the list of grandchildren he kept in the bible: Twins born to Justine and Kálmán, Sunday, December 21st, 1952. Anikó, 3:00 p.m. Four pounds and one ounce. Andorina, 3:10 p.m, Three pounds, 15 ounces.

A week after their birth, Mother brought my twin sisters home from the hospital and carefully laid the tiny bundles on her bed. They were so small! They didn't move or make a sound, and their eyes were closed. I backed away from the bed, afraid they were dead. Mom said she'd need our help and asked Andrea and me to choose.

Andrea, of course, was thrilled at the prospect of playing big sister and immediately asked, "Which one is bigger?"

Mother told her it was Anikó, and Andrea declared that Anikó was going to be her twin.

I just stood there helplessly looking at the silent babies. I couldn't imagine how they grew in Mom's tummy and then just popped out.

Mother told Andrea and me to sit on the end of her bed. She gently lifted baby Anikó and put her into Andrea's arms. I immediately sat on my hands. Mother lifted Andorina and cradled the tiny bundle protectively.

Looking at me, Mom quietly said, "This one is going to need more care. She's so small, the doctor doesn't know if she'll survive. She's very special, András, and needs the love and protection of a big brother."

I turned to face Andrea, "I wanted the little one anyway."

Mom smiled as I reluctantly pulled my hands out from under me and reached for Andorina.

By the end of their first year, in December of 1953, the twins were very healthy and extremely active. They looked so much alike! If it weren't for the different colored ribbons we put in their hair, green for Anikó and blue for Andorina, even we couldn't tell them apart. Mrs. Nagy ignored them except when they made too much noise, and Grandfather constantly got them confused. The twins weren't the only thing that confused Grandfather these days. Mother would give him money to buy groceries, and he'd be gone for hours, returning without food and without the money. When Mom asked him what he did with the money, Grandfather would look at her with his kind eyes and say, "I don't know. I got on the bus at Petőfi Square."

She'd ask him where he went, and he'd look surprised and answer, "I don't know." He was becoming more and more forgetful, and on several occasions, Mom had to search for him and bring him home.

Mother worked in a coffee shop while the twins were in daycare. Andrea and I made a habit of stopping at the cafe after school. I loved going into the warm shop during the bitter cold winter months. The smell of hot coffee, freshly baked pastries, and Mother's smile greeted us every afternoon as we walked through the door. Andrea and I would hop on the stools at the end of the counter, and Mom would give each of us a steaming mug of hot chocolate. The manager allowed us to stay just long enough to finish our drinks. If we lingered longer than she thought was necessary, she'd march over to Andrea and me, look in our mugs and say, "All right you two, move along now. Our customers don't like sharing the counter with kids."

The manager was a skinny woman with raven black hair. She always wore bright red lipstick and powdered her face white. Andrea said she looked like a clown. I thought she looked more like a witch. I got so mad at her once for rushing us out of the shop that the next day at school, I promised every kid in my class a free mug of hot chocolate if they'd show up at the cafe. When they stormed into the shop, the manager was so surprised and angry that for once, she was speechless. She kept working her jaw and moving her red lips but nothing came out.

The kids didn't actually break anything, but they refused to leave. They made so much noise that the witch had to give each of them not only a mug of hot chocolate but a pastry as well! Free! Mom almost got fired and gave me a terrible scolding that night, but everytime she paused to take a breath, she'd giggle.

The following afternoon Mother made me apologize to the manager who made me promise to kill myself if I ever did anything like that again. Andrea and I weren't allowed to set foot in the shop for a whole month afterwards, but it was worth it.

It took Mother thirteen months to find out where the secret police were keeping Dad. Once a week she'd go to their headquarters in the center of the city and ask them about Father. Grandma Margít often went with Mom, but even her grand lady voice and appearance didn't help. Mom never gave up though. She was such a frequent visitor at headquarters that the guards at the door and the sergeant at the front desk greeted her by name. Mom sometimes took the twins with her, hoping the sergeant would feel guilty and tell her where Dad was. She'd tell him all she wanted to do was send pictures of the twins to Dad and tearfully explained that he'd never seen his baby daughters. The sergeant, a young Hungarian Communist who'd been with the secret police for less than two years, was very kind but told her he didn't have access to information about prisoners.

Then one day, standing next to the front desk at headquarters and holding the twins in her arms, Mom suddenly handed Andorina over to the sergeant. He was so surprised he almost dropped her! Holding her gently, he cradled her in his arms. When Andorina smiled at him, his eyes welled up with tears, and he told Mom that his wife had given birth to their first child three weeks ago. The sergeant handed Andorina back to Mother and in a low whisper told her to come back in ten days, he'd get the information for her.

Ten days later in December of 1953, we learned that Father was still in Budapest. He was being kept at the Ferenci prison just a few miles from our apartment. The next day Mom and Grandma Margít went to the prison.

Mother walked into the apartment that night after picking up the twins from daycare, hurriedly set them down and left, promising she'd be back in twenty minutes. Andrea and I just looked at each other. We didn't have much time to guess what Mother was up to, because the twins immediately began crawling in different directions.

When Mom came home she had a grocery sack full of food we hadn't seen in weeks; three eggs, sliced ham, a can of peas, chocolate and even two apples! Andrea and I, each holding a twin, watched in amazement as Mom unpacked the food in the kitchen. Mother turned to us with a big smile, "Tonight we celebrate! I'm making ham and eggs for dinner. Andrea, go get Grandpa. András, put the twins in their highchairs and slice some bread."

I jumped into action, securing the twins in their chairs and giving each of them an apple to play with. They'd never seen an apple before! Mom began to sing as she started cooking. Andrea, Grandfather and I kept asking her questions about her trip to the prison, but she refused to tell us anything.

"Wait until you have some food in your stomachs!" was all she would say.

When we sat down to dinner, Mother finally told us that she'd been allowed to visit with Dad for ten minutes.

"He looked fine, a little thinner but fine. He told me he had been convicted of hiding Emil and sentenced to death, but later the sentence was changed to life in prison, then to 25 years. and just two months ago they changed the sentence to 15 years."

She said all this with so much joy that I stopped eating and looked at Andrea. Her fork was frozen in mid-air. Grandfather was nodding his head.

"Mom," I began hesitantly, "are you saying that Dad is going to be in prison for 15 years!"

"Yes! Isn't that wonderful! And the best part is it looks like they'll keep him right here in the city!" she replied with a smile.

"But Mother! I'll be twenty-five years old by the time Dad gets out!" Andrea exclaimed.

As Mom turned toward Andrea her smiled vanished. "Your father is alive. He wasn't sent to a labor camp. He isn't in prison for life. That's a lot to be thankful for."

Andrea dropped her fork on her plate and stared at Mother.

"Can we go visit him?" I asked, eager to break the tension.

"No," Mom replied quietly. "Children five years and older are not allowed into the prison."

Andrea and I stared at her in disbelief. My brain couldn't register what Mom just said.

"Visitors are only allowed once every three months and then, only if your father..." Mother paused, then continued slowly, "...only if he obeys all the rules. He'll have to be a model prisoner to have visitation rights." Mom folded her hands. When she resumed, her voice was a monotone, as if she were reading the regulations for the hundredth time. "Visits are restricted to twenty minutes each. There is to be no touching through the wire mesh. Food and gifts are not allowed. Grandma Margít and I will take turns. She'll see him next March, and I'll go in June." Mom's eyes scanned our blank faces. "If you want, you can come with me during my visits and wait outside. That way I can tell you about your father and give you his messages right away."

Andrea turned from Mother and stared at her plate. "You can only see him twice a year...for a total of forty minutes?"

I looked at Andrea. "And we won't see him for fifteen years." Andrea lifted her eyes and met my gaze. Grandfather slowly shook his head.

"I don't know which is more cruel."

As Andrea, Mom and I walked down the street after one of her visits with Dad, Mother jammed her hands deep into her coat pockets. She started walking so fast that Andrea and I had to run to keep up with her. Andrea shouted at her to slow down, but Mom didn't hear her or maybe she didn't want to hear her. I trotted along, amazed by the speed at which Mother was moving. After several blocks she suddenly stopped, turned, and waited for Andrea and me to catch up with her. Mom grabbed our hands and started walking at a moderately slower pace. I was so out of breath I couldn't say anything for several minutes. Andrea glared at Mom for a long time.

"Look around you," Mom said quietly. "Look at the buildings András. What color are they?"

I thought she was joking so I replied, "Purple, pink and yellow."

Mother stopped abruptly and glared down at me. I quickly looked at the shops, apartments, office buildings and turned to face her, "Gray except for the red stars."

All of the office buildings had the red star of the Soviet Union attached to them, either above the entrance to the building or on the roof. Some of the red stars on the roofs of the buildings were huge! I never paid much attention to them because they were everywhere, in all of the classrooms at school and in the middle of the red, white and green stripes of our national flags. These red stars were meant to remind us constantly that our country was controlled by the Communists.

Mom started walking again and asked, "Andrea, what color are the clothes of the people passing us?"

"Well Mom," Andrea began, "they're the same as always, dark blue, black, gray, dark green and brown."

"András," Mom continued, "what color are the cars on the street?"

I was beginning to think Mother had suddenly gone color-blind or perhaps her brain wasn't getting enough oxygen after walking so fast. I looked at the parked cars and announced their colors as we passed them, "Black, black, gray, black, gray, gray..."

Mom interrupted me, "It's all the same, the cars, the buildings, clothes. Gray, black, dark blue."

"What's the point, Mom?" Andrea demanded, "I see this every day!"

"That's exactly the point!" exclaimed Mother. "You don't see pink and yellow or lime green and purple or soft light blue. You don't have a single dress or skirt or blouse that isn't black, gray, white or dark blue."

I shook my head wondering what had brought this on when Mother announced, "You're growing up in a world without color, joy or enough to eat. You deserve better. We're not going to stay here. Some day we're all going to leave."

"Leave all these wonderfully drab colors? Mother, I couldn't!" I exclaimed jokingly.

40

Andrea frowned at me and asked, "You mean leave the city?"

Mother stopped and faced us, "No, I mean leave the country," she said quietly. "We're going to escape!"

"Escape?" I whispered loudly. A flood of questions tumbled from my mouth. "Where would we go? How could we leave the city? You know they won't let anyone out of the city without the proper permits. We can't just get on a train and cross the border! And what about Dad?"

Mother told me to be quiet, and she never mentioned leaving to us again, that is, until two years later when the city was being destroyed by Russian tanks, and soldiers were shooting everyone in sight. That's when Mother talked about escaping again.

CHAPTER SIX

SHOUTS FOR FREEDOM

The shooting started on October 23rd in 1956. I was eleven years old, Andrea was thirteen, and the twins were almost four years old.

For the past two days, huge groups of Hungarians had been gathering and making speeches all over the city. Mom said it was crazy. The government had a law that strictly forbade groups of three or more people from meeting. She thought they'd all be arrested and thrown in prison.

But it was so exciting! I'd never seen so many people gathered in one place. It was like a rally. Everyone was tense and excited at the same time!

The day before, as Andrea and I walked home from school and turned the corner at our street, we were almost knocked down by a crowd of college students from the nearby university. We tried to dodge the surging mass of people but it was like trying to swim against a raging river.

I grabbed Andrea's hand, allowing us to be swept up by the current of the crowd. I didn't know where we were going or what was going to happen. It didn't matter. I was excited and thrilled to be a part of the crowd. I picked up my pace and fell into step with the people walking beside me. We marched with the group to the Petőfi Square which was just a few blocks from home, next to the Danube river.

Thousands of people were there and everyone was shouting and chanting about freedom. Someone yelled something about freedom in the universities, and in the press; freedom of speech and worship. Most of all, the crowd was shouting, "the Russians must go."

As we stood on the park bench in the crowded square, I began to realize what they were shouting about. I looked over at Andrea. Her face was set as she listened intently to the shouts and demands of the crowd. I urgently pulled her arm to get her attention, "They want colors!" I yelled at her.

"What are you talking about?" she yelled back.

"Colors! Remember when Mom made us tell her the color of everything on the street?" I said, rushing my words together. "That's what they want to change, they want purples and blues, and pinks and yellows!"

Andrea squeezed my hand and excitedly said, "Yes! Colors!"

A young man was standing on the base of the statue of Sándor Petőfi in the middle of the square. Petőfi was a poet who died a long time ago. Mom once told us that Petőfi wrote a lot of love poems but that his most famous poem was about freedom for the country.

The man standing on the statue was reading a list of demands. He was dressed in a thin brown sweater and black pants. His voice shook as he spoke. I wasn't really listening to what he was saying. Instead, I watched the people in the square. The size of the crowd was amazing. I looked across the wide streets which led to the small square. People were coming out of shops and restaurants, leaning out of windows, and standing on the sidewalks. It was astonishing and forbidden!

Andrea grabbed my shoulder roughly, "Did you hear that?"

"What?" I asked bewildered.

"He said," she blurted and pointed to the man standing on the statue, "'all political prisoners should be released!'"

She stared at me expectantly, but her words didn't mean anything to my brain, already crowded with the images I was seeing.

"András! Listen to me!" Andrea said shaking me again, "He's talking about Dad!"

"Dad?" I asked, trying to focus my attention.

"Yes, you idiot! He's saying Dad and Emil and a bunch of other men in prison should be set free!" Andrea's eyebrows shot up in a questioning look.

I turned back toward the center of the square and shouted as loudly as I could, "Freedom for my father!" Andrea slapped her hand over my mouth. I couldn't tell if she was angry or scared. She took her hand away but kept her eyes on me. I rubbed my mouth with my fingers and yelled, "Freedom for my father."

Someone standing near us yelled, "Freedom for all fathers!" Others standing near us began to chant, "Freedom for all fathers!" And then voices throughout the crowd exploded in a tremendous noise.

Everyone in the square was shouting, "Freedom for all fathers!"

The crowd was so loud, it was deafening. The words rang out over and over again. The images and the people became a blur, and I felt myself filled with a joy I had never experienced.

Our shouts were suddenly pierced by the shrill sound of sirens. The crowd in the square quieted immediately and all heads turned toward the threatening wail of the approaching sirens. The people started moving away from the square and toward the safety of the streets and buildings nearby. Andrea grabbed my hand as we jumped off the park bench. A tall young man who had been standing near us grabbed Andrea by the arm, pulling her toward the nearest street. The crush of bodies was suffocating. As we reached the cafe on the street corner, the young man pushed us against the building and quickly asked us where we lived. People were running frantically in every direction. A stocky, dark haired man fell hard onto the pavement in front of me, scrambled to his feet and swayed unsteadily. I glanced back toward the square. The man who had been giving the speech was still standing on the statue, reading from the papers in his hands. Seven policemen quickly closed in on him.

I was jerked away from the building so roughly I almost fell into the throngs of rushing feet.

"Hurry up!" the young man yelled as he pulled Andrea and me along the street. I gasped for air as I tried to avoid colliding with the frenzied crowd. The stranger's grasp on my wrist felt like an iron claw. Shielding us with his body, he deftly moved up the narrow street, firmly pulling us behind him. We reached our apartment building in a matter of minutes. He yelled at us to hurry inside and immediately disappeared into the rush of bodies.

Andrea and I dashed into the building and stopped in the wide entry to catch our breath. We looked at each other and smiled. The next day the shooting started.

CHAPTER SEVEN

EXPLODING GUNFIRE

It happened right after dinner. Mom was sitting on the sofa mending a sweater. Andrea and I were playing with the twins. They were getting so big! It was hard to imagine how small they were four years ago. Grandfather sat on Mom's bed watching us. Suddenly Mother jerked her head toward the windows.

"What is it, Justine?" Grandpa asked.

Then all of us heard muted popping sounds. I listened carefully, guessing that the sound was reaching us from one or two streets away. I looked at Mom expectantly, not knowing what the sounds meant.

"Everybody, get down on the floor!" Mother ordered. She grabbed the twins and crawled toward the far end of the room.

Andrea quickly joined her. I craned my neck in the direction of the windows.

"András!" Mom yelled. "Get down and away from the windows."

"But what is it, Mom?"

"Gunfire. They're shooting." she replied matter-of-factly.

"Shooting? Who's shooting?" I demanded more out of astonishment than fear.

Andrea was lying on her side, Anikó in her protective arms. Grandfather was on all fours making his way slowly toward the door.

"Mom, who's shooting?" Andrea asked as she watched Grandpa reach for the door knob.

We heard a loud burst of gunfire and several single shots in reply.

"I'm not sure..." Mom began hesitantly. "That meeting you went to yesterday in the Petőfi Square...a much larger group met there early this afternoon. I was taking the bus to meet Uncle László. When the driver turned to go to the stop at the square, we were suddenly surrounded by hundreds of people. The street was so crammed, not even a bicyclist could get through. The driver tried to back up, but a throng of angry people behind the bus were pushing toward the square. We were stuck. The bus driver opened the door so we could hear. The crowd was insisting they be allowed to read their demands over the radio. There were so many people! Thousands of them! All of a sudden they started marching toward the Danube. They crossed the river on the Elizabeth Bridge. The entire span of the bridge was packed with people from one end to the other."

"So who's shooting?" I asked impatiently.

"I saw that same crowd marching along Rákóci Street at six this evening when I went to pick up the twins." Mother replied quietly. "I think the secret police must have become alarmed by the crowd."

"You mean the secret police are shooting the protestors?" Andrea asked.

"Yes. But it sounds like they're shooting back."

Just then Grandfather, hurried back into the room. He had Mom's small radio in his hand. Crawling over to her, he fumbled with the dials until he got a clear signal. An

48

announcer was telling everyone to stay out of the streets. Mom grabbed Grandfather's hand.

"We have taken over the radio station and are fighting to gain control of the Russian military headquarters. The army has been put on alert and told to shoot everyone on sight. Stay indoors."

"It's a revolution," Grandfather said sadly.

The headquarters of the secret police was just three blocks from our building! A beautiful old hotel, the Astoria, had been seized by the Russian military several years ago. The Astoria was five stories high with elegantly furnished rooms and an elaborate lobby. Mom said the hundreds of Russian soldiers who moved in there had destroyed the beauty of the fashionable hotel by tearing down walls, putting bars on the windows and wrecking the antique furniture.

The sound of gunfire became more sporadic as the evening wore on. Mother decided it was safe for us to get up and go to bed. She quickly changed the twins into their pajamas and told Andrea and me that no matter what we heard, to stay in our beds. Mom left the door to our room open, and sat at the kitchen table with the radio on.

"Andrea," I whispered, "Do you think there'll be fighting on our street?"

"How am I supposed to know that, dummy? Maybe. Be quiet and go to sleep."

"But do you think we might see some people getting shot?" I asked hopefully.

"András, you're crazy if you want to see people getting shot! This isn't like a game you and your stupid friends play. There are probably hundreds of people lying dead in the streets right now, and others bleeding to death."

"Well, if they're secret police or soldiers that's good!" I declared and then shuddered at the sudden image in my mind of bullets piercing the chest a of man with blood red stripes on his collar. I turned my face to the wall and saw myself holding the gun.

The next morning as I rolled off the sofa and stretched sleepily on the floor, Andorina ran over to me and sat on my legs. She had an expectant look in her bright green eyes.

"Okay, okay," I moaned and lifted her high above my chest. She giggled, flapping her arms and legs. "That's it, Rina, I have to get ready for school." I sat her on the floor next to me. I looked at Andrea's empty cot. She was probably already dressed, had finished breakfast and was reviewing her homework in the kitchen. *Why did she always have to be so obedient?*

"No," Andorina said shaking her head vigorously.

"Yes, I do, and you can help me fold the blankets."

"No! No school."

"Yes, I have to go," I replied more firmly and stood up.

"No school!" she shouted.

Too sleepy to stand there and argue, I grabbed my blankets.

"No school!" she repeated as loudly as before.

I was about to reply when Mom came in. "Andorina, stop shouting and go finish your breakfast."

50

Andorina scurried to her feet and looked me in the eye, "No school," she ordered.

"Yeah, right."

"She's right, András," Mom said as she came over to help me with the blankets.

"No school?"

"Early this morning, the radio announced that all schools were closed. There's still a lot of shooting in the city." Mother nodded her head toward the street.

"Who's winning?"

"I don't know."

I stopped folding my blankets and faced her with a flood of questions, "How long do you think the fighting will last? Have a lot of people been shot? Will they fight on our street? How..."

"András!" Mother exclaimed. "You're asking too many questions again! I don't know the answers." She continued quietly, "All we can do is listen to the radio. Most of the fighting is in this area."

Mother sat down on the sofa. " I don't know how long this will last or what's going to happen. I just want to make sure all of you are safe, so I've made some decisions. I'm going to take the twins to Grandma Margít's as soon as they finish breakfast. They'll be safer in the suburbs of Buda with her. I'm sending Andrea to the country, a boarding school in Bakony. I know the principal. He'll take her in. Grandfather will take her on the train. I just hope he doesn't get confused and loose his way home." Mom sighed, then straightened her shoulders and stood up.

51

I rushed to ask the questions piling up in my brain, "But aren't you afraid you'll get shot at? Andrea and Grandfather might not even make it to the train station! How can you send them out into the streets?"

"Stop asking questions, András! I haven't slept, and I have no patience!" Mom grabbed the last blanket and started folding it.

"The fighting is just going to get worse. I have to get the girls to a safer place. Most of the shooting is several blocks from here, away from the river, so we should get to Grandma Margít's house okay. The radio said the buses are not running so we'll have to walk. No fighting has been reported near the train station yet. Grandfather and Andrea should make it all right."

I turned away from her. It was too dangerous! I felt hot tears filling my eyes.

"I have to go," Mother said and started toward the kitchen.

"What about me?" I whispered through my tears.

Mom stopped in the doorway, "I need you to stay here, András. I tried to call Uncle László this morning, but no one answered. He may be on his way here. I don't know, but someone needs to stay in the apartment. Go wash up and get dressed." With that she turned and walked out of the room.

It was a little before 8:00 a.m. when they left.

"I should be back in two or three hours," Mom stated as she hurried out holding the twins' hands.

I walked through every room in the apartment, opening all of the doors. Mrs. Nagy hadn't come home last night. Mom said she was probably still at the restaurant.

I walked back to our room and sat on the window sill. There were people on the sidewalks and a couple of cars in the street. It looked so normal! I saw the lights come on in the window directly across from our apartment. The massive, gray, five-story building across the street housed the main post office in Pest. Workers were making their way to their offices as if it were just another day. I gazed toward the intersection of Petőfi and Párisi streets. Located on the ground floors of the large, old buildings were a clothing shop and an electronics store. One of the young women who worked at the clothing shop was washing the display window, just as she did every morning.

I heard gunfire nearby. My eyes darted down to the street.

The woman washing the window stopped, cocked her head for a moment, then continued her chore. Two men on the sidewalk didn't even break stride at the sound of shooting.

I jerked my head up as I heard a loud knock on the front door. Péter's mother, Erzsí, smiled tensely as I let her in.

"Hello, András. You know there's no school today."

"I know. We heard it on the radio."

"I don't understand," she continued nervously, "Péter always listens to the radio in the morning. Maybe he didn't hear the announcement. He left earlier than usual for school. It's only five blocks away. He should have been home by now. Surely he saw that it was closed."

"Didn't he come back?" I asked.

"No. Where's your mother?"

"She took the twins to Grandma's."

Erzsí looked around, as if she'd forgotten why she came. She finally spoke, "Thanks, András. I'll go back to the apartment and wait for Péter."

"Okay. Tell him to come over when he gets home."

I closed the door, wondering why Péter went to school. He always listened to the radio. There's no way he could have missed the announcement.

An hour later Péter's mother reappeared. Her eyes were wild with panic.

"He's still not home!" Her hands were locked in fists under her chin. "Did he call here?"

"No." Péter's family didn't have a telephone and would use ours occasionally.

"I can't sit and wait any more. I have to go look for him!"

"I'm going with you!" I said, grabbing my jacket off of the coatrack in the entry. I rushed out the door before she could change her mind.

As we hurried down the sidewalk, I heard gunfire before we reached the end of the block. There were at least a dozen people walking quickly along the street. Some of the men were carrying briefcases, and one woman had a grocery sack in her arms. They didn't pay any attention to us as we hurried toward the school.

We turned the corner onto Kossuth Street and immediately flattened ourselves against the cold gray wall. A man with a rifle was standing in the doorway of the stationery store just around the corner from us. I moved to the edge of the wall and peered down the street. The man with the rifle was still there. He was shooting at a third floor window of the building across the way. I saw the gunman in the window take aim with his machine gun, fire a round and miss. Shots were suddenly fired from several of the tall buildings surrounding the wide intersection. I crouched down, my eyes searching the buildings.

Startled by a heavy weight on my back, I quickly spun around. Péter's mom leaned against me as she pointed down the street. A group of men and boys were tearing up the cobblestones from the street with their bare hands and throwing them onto an already large pile. A trolley car was turned on its side next to the pile of stones. Three men stood behind the trolley with rifles at their shoulders. They were aiming at the roof of the building nearest them. An old woman with a basket of vegetables stepped out of a doorway and walked in our direction. Her head was in constant motion following the gunfire, but there was no fear in her walk. She ducked into the doorway of a building when a burst of shots exploded around her.

I heard it before I saw it. A low rumbling and high-pitched whining sound. Something sounded like a noisy bicycle chain only much louder, more insistent. Then I saw the monstrous machine. A Russian tank, a red star painted on its side, turned onto the street in front of the Astoria Hotel. Like a drugged bulldog, its lolling head moving mechanically, the tank rolled forward slowly, its enormous gun swinging from side-to-side.

Stopping at the intersection just ten yards in front of us, the gun began its slow, smooth turn toward the barricade the men were building with the cobblestones and disabled trolley car. The man in the doorway of the store yelled at his fellow Freedom Fighters down the street to get away from the barricade.

Suddenly, a deafening blast shot out from the powerful tank. I clapped my hands over my ears. The trolley car exploded. The force of the blast sent huge pieces of metal flying high into the air. A man's limp body landed hard in the middle of the street.

The second blast from the tank destroyed the pile of cobblestones, which flew like pebbles, then dropped hard, slamming against buildings and shattering windows.

The terrified fighters building the barricade scattered. The tank fired its powerful gun one more time before confidently turning toward the stationery store.

I scooted back a few feet and jumped. Erzsí grabbed my hand, and we raced down our street. I turned my head and saw the tank retreat. We covered the long city block in a matter of seconds, rounded the corner and collapsed on the sidewalk trying to catch our breath. A few people hurried along the street. Erzsí stood, pulling me up with her. It was quiet.

Pointing a shaky finger in the direction of the Danube, "Maybe we can get around the shooting and get to the school this way," she said with a mixture of hope and fear.

I nodded in reply, too stunned to speak.

We ran several blocks, circling back toward the high school before being stopped by fierce gunfire. The school was just one block away!

Five men ran past us, their guns held lightly in front of them. We dashed into the doorway of a flower shop and bumped into an older couple hidden in the shadows.

"Careful there! I may need these feet soon," the stranger said as I jumped off of his left foot and apologized. He smiled at me and patted me on the back.

As he stepped away from the doorway, I noticed the strength in his body. His movements were deliberate and powerful. He looked down the street, then signaled to the woman. Taking her hand as she reached for him, they walked away quickly without looking back.

I glanced down the street. "If we go up another two blocks we might be able to get to the school from University Street."

Erzsí shook her head. "It's no use. There's too much shooting near the school. We'd better get back to the apartment."

We walked back to her apartment in silence. Péter wasn't there. I went downstairs unsure if Mother would ever return.

Mother came home shortly after one o'clock. I rushed to hug her and immediately asked, "How'd you get past the shooting?"

She looked down at me. "The twins are safe," was all she said. She walked to the kitchen and turned on the radio.

Following quickly behind, I told her Péter's mom had come over and said he was missing. I wanted to tell Mother about our unsuccessful search for him but forced myself to keep quiet, realizing that it would only convince her I couldn't be trusted to do as I was told.

Grandfather walked through the door three hours later, said he'd left Andrea in good hands and went to his bedroom. Mom followed him but stepped back into our room seconds later.

"He's going to lie down for a while. I'll go fix something to eat."

I nodded and picked up the book in my lap, but my mind kept replaying the fighting I witnessed this morning. The sound of sporadic gunfire penetrated the double-paned windows of the apartment. I closed my eyes, waking up an hour later to the shrill ring of the telephone.

Mom answered it. "Your mother's been worried sick, Péter." I sprang from the sofa and stood directly in front of Mom.

"Okay, I'll tell her." Mom hung up and looked at me.

"Péter's safe," she said, "He's staying at a friend's house and can't make it home with all the shooting going on. I'd better go tell Erzsí."

Four days later Péter came home carrying a rifle.

CHAPTER EIGHT

RELEASED FROM PRISON

Mother, Grandpa and I sat in the kitchen eating lunch and listening to the radio. Seven incredible days had passed since the shooting started.

"Attention, attention," the announcer's voice suddenly boomed from the small radio. "Today, October 29th, at 1:00 o'clock, we, the free people of Hungary, have gained control of the city. The daily newspaper, proclaiming our victory and outlining the future for our country, will be distributed in the streets at 6:00 p.m. God bless us."

We sat speechless as the announcer started reading a list of the areas in the city that were now safe. Some skirmishes between the Russians and Freedom Fighters continued in parts of the city and in the outskirts. These would soon cease, he said confidently.

I jumped up and ran to the windows in our room. Mother and Grandfather hurried to stand beside me. People were streaming out of buildings, hugging each other and smiling. A group of boys waved the red, white and green Hungarian flag which had a large hole in the middle of it where someone had cut out the despised red star. The excitement in the street surged through my body. Turning to Mom I eagerly asked, "Can I go? Please?"

"Yes, but don't go too far from Petőfi Street and be back before dark."

I rushed to grab my jacket and took the stairs two at a time. Bursting into the street, I scanned the crowd, caught sight of a boy from my class and hurried to join him. We hugged each other like long lost friends and fell into step with the crowd. A lone, deep voice rose in the mass of joyous people and began singing the first few bars of the national anthem. Hundreds of voices joined in. We walked with confidence. Our voices filled with pride. As we marched pasted the Astoria Hotel, we sang louder, with more determination and hope. It was fantastic! People everywhere were hurrying to join us. Thousands of people filled the street! Total strangers patted me on the head and some of them even hugged me. I had never experienced such happiness.

Returning to our apartment building several hours later, I slowly started up the stairs. I felt the same mixture of excitement and exhaustion as I did five days ago when Erzsí and I went to look for Péter. Then, what I had seen was the tank blowing up the trolley car. The difference, I suddenly realized was that the excitement and exhaustion I now felt came from an unspeakable joy, whereas five days ago, it came from having been totally terrified.

Voices were coming from the kitchen as I entered our apartment and hung up my jacket. Reaching the open door of the kitchen I couldn't believe what I saw.

"Dad!" I yelled, running to him.

Pulling me into his arms, Dad hugged me hard and showered my face with kisses. Turning my head toward Mother I saw a wondrous smile.

"Dad, how did you..." I began in a rush, but Mom interrupted me.

"I know you have a million questions, András, but save your breath and just listen, all right?"

I reluctantly closed my mouth and sat next to Grandpa. Dad looked at me with tired eyes.

"There isn't much to tell, András. Around ten o'clock this morning all of the prison guards were suddenly called away from their posts. We heard the intense fighting outside and assumed the guards were needed to protect the building. By noon it was quiet. Thirty minutes later, three Freedom Fighters with rifles slung over their shoulders came into our section of the prison. They explained that they couldn't just open the cell doors and let everybody go. One of them said, 'We want to make absolutely certain that only those of you who are political prisoners are released. Common criminals, those of you who are murderers and thieves, are staying.' He told us that a group of six people were in the process of reviewing everybody's file, starting at the beginning of the alphabet. I was released at 4:30 p.m."

I took a deep breath and exhaled loudly. Looking at Dad, I realized how thin he was. His cheekbones stood out at sharp angles, and his arms were very skinny. I was desperate to ask him what prison was like but bit back my questions.

Mom stood up and began making dinner.

"Kálmán, I apologize but all we have are a few potatoes and some butter."

We could still hear people celebrating in the street as we finished dinner. Mom had gone downstairs to get a newspaper, and now she and Dad were reading it intently. The small radio sitting on the kitchen counter was turned on low. When the announcer stated he had a bulletin, Father grabbed it and turned up the volume immediately.

61

"Fellow trusted people of this great nation, we have sent a plea for help to the free countries of the world. We are requesting their assistance in ridding our nation of all Communists."

Father abruptly turned the radio off and shook his head.

"If we don't get help from the West, from America, Britain and France, within the next few days, the Russians will mobilize their troops again. They say they're withdrawing from the country, but thousands of their tanks and soldiers are waiting just outside of our borders!" Dad pushed himself away from the table and stood up. "We must have help or the Russians will come in and crush us!"

Pausing to control his anger, Dad sighed, "Come on, I haven't seen the city in four years, let's take a walk."

Grandfather decided not to join us as Mother, Dad and I pulled on our coats and caps.

We walked down Petőfi Street toward the Astoria Hotel on Kossuth Boulevard. Groups of people were walking in the same direction. Nearing the empty, bullet scarred Russian headquarters, I noticed a blazing fire in front of the building. As we approached, I saw a dozen people running in and out of the building directly across from the Astoria, feeding the bonfire.

"That's the Communist bookstore!" Mother exclaimed.

When the Communists took control of Hungary after World War II, thousands of books by both Hungarian and foreign authors were banned and burned. The history books that schools had used were all destroyed, and new ones were issued, written by the government. These omitted and distorted many events important to our country's history.

Father laughed as we reached the large fire. "Their lies put out a nice heat."

The three of us stood in the crowd watching and cheering as every book in the store was burned.

Péter knocked on our door late in the afternoon the following day. He looked like he hadn't slept or eaten in days.

"Does your mother know you're back?" Mom asked as she released him from a warm hug.

"Yes, of course. She told me your husband was also home."

Nodding, Mother led him into our room announcing, "Look who's here!"

"Péter! You're alive" I shouted rushing to him. Giving me a weak pat on the back, he turned toward father.

"I'm glad to see you, sir."

"I hear you've had some adventures yourself," Dad replied shaking his hand.

"Yes, and I need your help with something."

"What is it, Péter?"

"I need to get rid of a rifle."

Father nodded. "Tell me what happened."

Péter quickly looked at Mother, then sat down.

"On the 24th, when I heard that school was cancelled, I knew I couldn't just sit at home and do nothing. I had to join the fight against the Communists. So, I went to school. Thirty-five boys showed up. Mr. Takács, our gym teacher was there, and I don't know where he got them,

63

but he had a bunch of rifles and pistols.   We split into groups of five. Mr. Takács told my group to go one block past the Russian Headquarters, on Kossuth Boulevard, to the Áruház building. We went up the back way to the roof."

"You're a Freedom Fighter!" I said proudly.

Péter looked at me with expressionless eyes.

"Yes, but two of my best friends are dead, and so is Mr. Takács." Péter turned to Father.

"Mr. Takács was helping build the barricade on Kossúth Street when a tank blasted the trolley car they'd turned over."

My jaw dropped, and my eyes opened wide in horror.

"András, what is it?" Mother asked staring at me.

I stammered, trying to control my shock, "I uh...ah...Mr. Takács...I'm...I liked him a lot," I finally managed, resisting the temptation to reveal what I had seen.

"Péter, let's go get that rifle. If the Russians do attack the city, they'll do it with hundreds of tanks and thousands of soldiers. The rifle will be useless, and you could be executed if they find it."

Dad stood up and looked at me. "Do you want to come with us?"

Nodding, I moved slowly toward the entry to get my coat.

In Péter's apartment, Father disassembled the rifle and gave each of us various pieces to hide under our coats.

We walked down Párisi street to the shores of the Danube river and along its bank under the Elizabeth Bridge. Walking in silence, I stared at the bullet-riddled buildings we passed. Some buildings were totally destroyed. Others had large sections missing; gaping holes stared back at me. I was amazed at the destruction and wondered how I had missed it the other night when I was celebrating in the streets.

Chunks of stone and concrete littered the sidewalks. Disabled tanks, buses and cars were scattered along the street. Glass from windows and store fronts crunched under our feet. The bodies of Russian soldiers rotted inside the burned-out tanks and others were left exposed in the streets.

Walking along the river front, Father stopped near an empty bench, turned, and walked directly toward the fast flowing river. Péter and I followed without saying a word. Dad picked up a rock and tossed it far into the Danube. He casually turned and looked in all directions before pulling the butt of the rifle from under his coat and quickly throwing it into the river. Gazing at Péter and me, he indicated with a nod of his head for us to do the same.

Five days later, at 4:00am on a Sunday morning, it wasn't my Mother's gentle voice that awakened me, but the terrifying sound of low-flying airplanes and hundreds upon hundreds of Russian tanks thundering into Budapest.

CHAPTER NINE

OUR CITY SHATTERED

Everything shattered that Sunday morning. The sound of gunfire erupted around us in a deafening noise. Two thousand tanks crashed through the streets. The Russians were tearing the city apart, blasting buildings at random and shooting anyone who ventured outside. Heavy artillery guns shelled the city, landing with terrifying force. One hundred forty thousand soldiers with sub-machine guns swarmed like ants through the city, and low-flying planes dropped high explosive rockets. I was certain a bomb would hit our building and wondered what it was going to feel like. The shelling was constant. Twelve huge tanks rolled down our short street before noon.

Standing by the window of our room, I saw three people shot, their bodies left in the street. Two of the dead were women who'd been carrying empty shopping baskets. I was stunned. The Communists were slaughtering everyone in sight! I searched desperately for some emotion to register and fill my body, my mind, to let me know that what I was witnessing was real. No emotion penetrated the numbness of my shock at the rampage of death around us.

There was nowhere to go; nothing we could do. Leaving the window, I joined Mom and Dad in the kitchen. Father sat at the table with his arms folded in front of him. Still very thin, the skin on his prominent cheekbones was taut. His eyes expressed a mixture of anger and sadness. Mom had her hands in her lap, her shoulders hunched forward, eyes half closed. She broke the grim silence.

66

"I'm glad we decided to leave the twins with Grandma Margít awhile longer."

Father slowly nodded his head in agreement.

Mother took a deep breath, straightened her shoulders and looked directly at Dad. "Kálmán, we have to get out of here!"

Father looked up, their eyes locking.

"If we survive, we have to leave. I can't stay here, and I won't raise our children under the oppression of Communism. Not one of them will have the right to attend a high school or get a decent job. You know as well as I that we've been labeled enemies of the State, blacklisted because of our arrests and your imprisonment. None of them will have an opportunity to get an education. We have to escape!" Mom declared.

Father held her eyes with his for a moment, then slammed his fist on the table. "No! I won't leave my country! We're Hungarians! This is where we belong. This is our country! Besides, it's too dangerous. What if we did try to escape and one of the children was shot?"

"Then the other three would live in freedom," Mom replied quietly.

"We're not going! We can't go! What about your Father and László and his wife? My mother? We can't just leave them! The secret police will line them up and shoot them without hesitation. Do you want that on your conscience?"

Mother looked out the small kitchen window. Tanks were still rumbling down the street, blasting buildings randomly. She turned to Dad.

67

"I won't try to talk you into doing anything, and I won't leave without you. If you don't want to escape, we'll stay here." The resignation and sadness in her voice was unmistakable.

We stayed locked in the apartment for two weeks. Father ventured out occasionally, looking for what food he could find and any information he could get about the fighting. He wouldn't let Mother, Granddad or me leave the apartment. It was too dangerous.

The Freedom Fighters continued to fight that first week of November, but the pleas for help, broadcast to foreign countries everywhere, brought nothing. No one was willing to help us fight the Communists.

Father told us of the raging fires throughout the city and the looting by the soldiers who stole everything they could get their hands on. Conducting house-to-house searches for weapons, they shot anyone who was found to have a rifle or gun. The soldiers were arresting thousands of people, some because they had participated in the fighting, others just because they were out on the street. Forced onto freight trains like cattle, they were immediately taken to Russian labor camps.

Father explained that the Russians were trying to starve out any remaining rebels in the city and at the same time, force people back to work. But the entire country had declared a general strike as a way of rebelling against the Communists. Few fighters remained in the city, and they were losing. Their meager weapons were no match for the thousands of tanks and soldiers.

I was bored out of my mind sitting in the apartment day after day. Then, on November 18th, there was a knock

68

on the door. Dad opened the front door cautiously at first, then threw it wide and warmly embraced his close friend, Mr. Olivér and his wife.

Dad and Mr. Olivér met in the army and fought together during World War II. The Olivér's two children, a girl, Píri age nine and a boy, Árpád, age seven, weren't with them.

"When are we going?" Mr. Olivér asked before he had finished taking his coat off.

Father didn't respond until we were all seated in the kitchen. "We're not going. It's crazy even to think about it!"

"Well, we're going to escape," said Mr. Olivér, his round face expressing both eagerness and determination.

Mother, Mrs. Olivér and I sat silently watching the two men.

"Fine, go! But you'll never make it out! Your whole family will be slaughtered at the border!"

"Kálmán, listen to me," Mr. Olivér pleaded, "You and your family have to come with us. You can't stay here."

"No! We're not going."

It was like listening to two people talking to themselves. Each refused to hear the other, and each was firm in his conviction. Mom and Mrs. Olivér exchanged nervous glances. I knew how much Mother wanted to go, and this was the first real opportunity, perhaps the only one we would have. I sat on my hands and kept my mouth shut, but I was incredibly excited. Just the thought of getting out of the apartment thrilled me!

"You're crazy if you think you're going to make it out. All of you will be captured and arrested. If the Russians don't shoot you, they'll imprison you. You have no idea what they will do to you in prison!" Dad leaned back in his chair as he finished speaking. No one said a word.

Mr. Olivér nodded his head slightly and calmly said, "Kálmán, this is my country too. I want to stay, but I must think of my children. What kind of future can I give them here? I can teach them how to lie and cheat. I can teach them not to trust anyone." He shook his head. "No father should feel he has to teach such things to his child. This country is not ours, Kálmán. It belongs to the Communists. We've failed to free the country, now, we must think about freeing ourselves. Thousands of people are escaping. A lot of them are crossing the border into Austria. Yes, the Russians have hundreds of soldiers and guards in every village and city between here and the border. And yes, it's 125 miles from here, and no one can leave Budapest without the proper papers. There are checkpoints at every road leading out of the city and at all of the train stations." Mr. Olivér paused. "Kálmán, we have to at least try."

Dad didn't say anything for a long time. Mom stared at the table and Mrs. Olivér at her husband. I watched the expression on Dad's face change as he struggled to make a decision.

"I have friends in the construction industry. They told me the Russians are recruiting workers to go to the border city of Ács. They want the large sugar refinery there rebuilt as soon as possible. I think my friends would give me the necessary transfer papers stating you and I have been hired by their firm to help rebuild the refinery."

70

Mother's whole face lit up. Dad looked at us, not with a smile, but with a sense of resignation.

"Get the papers, Kálmán. I think I can get the truck we'll need to transport us to the border. I have a friend who works at a shipping plant on the outskirts of the city. I'll talk to him tomorrow," said Mr. Olivér.

I couldn't believe my ears! We were actually going to escape!

I sucked in my lower lip to keep myself from shouting with joy. Mother glanced at me and smiled. She lifted her hand and gently placed her forefinger to her lips.

Mom knew I was about to ask a million questions. I returned my attention to Father.

"If we get caught within the city limits," he said, looking Mr. Olivér directly in the eyes, "they'll probably just arrest us. If we make it to the border and get caught there, they'll probably shoot us."

CHAPTER TEN

ABANDONING OUR HOME

Dad and Mr. Olivér calculated they could get the truck and the transfer papers within a day or two and set Tuesday, November 20, as the day we would leave Budapest. They talked for hours, discussing every detail of the escape and every terrifying possibility should it fail.

One of Dad's main concerns was the number of people we were planning to take. There was Mr. and Mrs. Olivér, their two children, Mom, Dad, Grandfather, Grandmother, Andrea, me, the twins and a friend of Dad's from prison named Ródi. Thirteen people on a truck, six of them children. Dad knew the soldiers would be very suspicious, even with the proper transit papers. It was a chance we'd have to take. No one was going to be left behind.

After Mr. and Mrs. Olivér left, Mom slipped her arms around Dad and quietly said, "Thank you."

Father ran his hands through his short, brown hair and rubbed the back of his neck. "I don't know, Justine. I just don't know. If we're stopped and they question me, what am I going to say about being in prison, because you know they'll ask! If I lie and they check their records, they'll shoot me immediately, and all of you will be deported to labor camps."

Mom sat down and looked Dad straight in the eyes. "I know we're taking an enormous risk, not just with our own lives but with those of our children and our parents. But I can't live in a world anymore where I'm always afraid.... afraid of strangers on the street, afraid of what I can or can't say to my friends, afraid that I can't get enough food for my children. I can't live in a world where I have to lie to my children in order to protect them."

Dad nodded his head. "I had to tell so many lies in prison just to survive." He reached his hand out to hers. I folded my arms on the table, wondering what Mom had lied about to me.

"Justine," Dad began, "do you really think your father is well enough to make the trip?"

"His health is fine...it's his mind. I think if we just tell him we're going on an excursion, he'll be okay. He's like a child, he'll do whatever I ask of him." Mom hesitated a moment before asking, "And your mother?"

Dad shrugged his shoulders. "I don't think she'll go." He paused and shook his head. "In fact, I know she won't leave, not the way we're planning to. The idea of escaping from her own country...there's only one way she'd go, and that's with her head held high. She's too proud and too old. It would take me days to try and talk her into it, and I know I'd fail. She won't go." He stopped and swallowed hard. "If it weren't for you and the children, I wouldn't go. I just don't know if I should even tell her that we're leaving. She may try to stop us."

"It'll break her heart to know she may never see her grandchildren again," Mom quietly said.

"Yes, I know," Dad sighed.

"Did I tell you that Laci and his wife might leave also?"

"No!" Dad looked at her in surprise.

"I spoke with him last week. He asked us to come along but, well...you...we decided not to leave. He didn't tell me

73

much except that he's waiting for Tibor to get back into town on Wednesday or Thursday. I'll call Laci tomorrow. I have to let him know we're going, and we have to find a way to contact each other once we've escaped."

Escaped! I formed the word silently with my mouth and saw us driving through barricades, shooting soldiers and triumphantly bursting through the border to freedom!

Monday morning I dressed quickly and started shoving socks and sweaters into my small canvas bag, preparing for tomorrow's journey.

"Take those out, András," Mom said when she saw what I was doing.

"But Mom, they're my favorite. I promise to carry the bag by myself all the way."

"That's not it, son. We have to leave everything except what we're wearing. Any type of bag or suitcase will alert the Russians that we're trying to escape."

I stared at my small bag, reluctant to pull anything out of it. "Can't we take anything, Mom?" I pleaded looking around at our few possessions in the room.

"No, nothing. I'll put the toothbrushes in my purse. That's it."

Father came home late that evening with the forged papers. I jumped in excitement as he pulled them from his coat pocket and showed the papers to Mother and me.

"How'd you get them?" I asked him eagerly.

"It's best that you and Mother don't know. If we're caught, you won't have to lie about it."

Mom nodded, then looked at me, "András, it's late, go to bed."

It was an order I was about to protest when I noticed the tension in her face. Leaving Mom and Dad reluctantly, I went to bed thinking of tomorrow's adventure.

But we didn't leave Tuesday. Mr. Olivér couldn't get the truck. Bitterly disappointed, I spent the day staring out the window.

It wasn't until 2:00 p.m. on Thursday, the 22nd, when Mr. Olivér anxiously knocked on our door.

"Ready?"

"Yes," Father replied, and the four of us, Mom, Dad, Grandfather and I hurried down the stairs to the flat-bed truck. Mrs. Olivér, their two children and Mr. Ródi were already sitting in the back of the truck. Mom, Granddad, Mr. Olivér and I quickly climbed on. Dad sat up front in the cab with the driver, and suddenly we were off.

The old truck bed was made of steel and Mrs. Olivér had put three bedspreads down for everyone to sit on. The sides of the truck were made of wood slats, two feet high all around. I pushed my back against the cold steel of the cab. No one spoke a word as we headed across the river to Grandmother Margít's house to get the twins.

Dad had not called Grandma to tell her he was picking up the twins or about our escape. Just as Mrs. Nagy had been moved into our apartment, the Communists had moved a whole family of strangers into Grandma's house. He was concerned that his phone call might be overheard.

Father instructed the driver to stop the truck one block from Grandma's house. Dad jumped out, whispered urgently for me to follow him and hurried up the street. When Grandma Margít answered the door, she was very surprised and hugged and kissed us both.

Dad, nervous and tense, didn't waste any time, refusing her invitation to come in for a cup of coffee. "Mom, get the twins, we're taking them to Mr. and Mrs. Verdes out in the country. They'll be safer there."

Grandmother was shocked. "What do you mean? Why didn't you call me about this?"

"Mother please, it's not safe for András and me to be on the streets, just get the girls quickly," Father replied tensely.

Grandmother hurried inside and shortly reappeared with Anikó and Andorina. I was so happy to see them! They ran into my arms kissing me and chattering excitedly.

Father hugged his Mother gently, "I love you," he said, then swept Anikó up into his arms and hurried away. I lifted Andorina and ran after him.

Setting the twins into the truck and scampering in after them, I watched the girls rush into Mother's arms. Holding them tightly, Mom showered them with kisses as tears slipped down her cheeks.

Giggling and squirming, Anikó and Andorina settled in on either side of Mother, her arms around them protectively.

"I have such a surprise for you two," Mother whispered.

The twins stared up at her anxiously.

"First, both of you have to promise me that you'll do exactly what I say."

They nodded their small, scarf-covered heads eagerly.

"We're taking a little trip to visit your big sister, Andrea!"

Anikó and Andorina squealed and clapped their hands in delight.

Mother smiled. "From now on, until we get to her boarding school, both of you must be very good girls and not talk except in a whisper, okay?"

"Okay, Mommy," Anikó replied happily.

"Okay, Mommy," Andorina imitated.

We were driving through the gently rolling hills of Buda. It was very cold sitting in the back of the truck, and a light drizzle was falling, but no one seemed to notice. Pulling myself up by the side of the truck, I kneeled, gazing at the city as we climbed through the winding hills. My heart thundered with the excitement of our secret journey!

Looking across the Danube toward Pest, my eyes drifted along the wide river toward the gray buildings lining its shores. All of the buildings had huge holes in their sides, and most of the windows were gone. The Russian tanks had destroyed so much of the city! Turning toward Mother, I saw her staring in the same direction and then noticed that all of the adults had their eyes fixed on the city. Their faces were expressionless. They looked blankly across the Danube. No one said a word as we left Budapest forever.

CHAPTER ELEVEN

A DANGEROUS ROAD

Reaching the outskirts of the city along a small, two-lane road, the truck slowed slightly. I peered through the window of the cab and saw the soldiers. There were two of them, dressed in long gray-blue coats with caps which partially hid their young faces. Each had a rifle slung over his shoulder. The driver stopped the truck.

Mother motioned to the twins to be quiet, firmly pressing a finger to her lips. The soldiers approached the cab slowly, their faces pinched from the cold. Both were very young and clean shaven.

"Papers!" one of them shouted. The other soldier grinned at him and leaned on the hood of the truck.

Dad handed over the papers without a word.

I looked over at Mr. and Mrs. Olivér. Sitting like statues, they stared into space. Huddled beside their parents, Piri and Árpád looked terrified. Mr. Ródi had his hands jammed deep inside his coat pockets and pretended to be asleep. The twins cuddled on either side of Mom, their faces buried in her arms. Looking at Mother, her thin brown hair covered tightly with a scarf, her lips tightly drawn, I saw the hardness in her eyes. I was astonished by the determined look on her face, and as I stared at her, I more fully understood her deep desire to escape.

The soldier holding the papers swayed slightly, his head bowed in concentration. His comrade laughed and said, "Come on, hurry up, I'm freezing! Quit trying to read every line, just make sure the government stamp is authentic and let's go!"

"Go around the side of the truck and check it out."

The soldier leaning on the hood ignored the order.

The one holding our precious papers yelled at him, "Hey, I gave you an order!"

"I'm too tired," the other replied as he pushed himself away from the truck.

"Do as you're told!" the soldier with the papers shouted. The second soldier began walking around the truck in a hurry, weaving as he went. He didn't even look at us!

As soon as he reached the other side of the cab, he slapped his comrade on the back and said, "Okay, give them the papers, and let's go before I freeze to death."

"I could report you for this!"

The soldier shrugged and started walking away.

Furious, the man holding the papers started marching after him. "Get back here!" he shouted repeatedly without results.

I kept my eyes on the papers clutched in his hand. We had to have them back! No one in the truck moved a muscle. Even the twins sat perfectly still. I held my breath. This couldn't be the end of our plans!

The soldier stopped abruptly. Turning toward the truck, he quickly moved toward the cab. Filled with rage, he looked at the driver and Father for a brief moment, uncertain what to do. He suddenly threw the papers into the open window.

"Get out of here!" he yelled at the driver, then stormed after his comrade.

Shifting gears, the driver slowly pulled away from the side of the road. Mother's shoulder's sagged as she breathed deeply. Mr. Olivér covered his round face with his hands. Opening his eyes slowly, Mr. Ródi clenched his teeth. No one spoke.

We reached Andrea's boarding school in Bakony three hours later. Mother had called the school at noon when we knew for certain that Mr. Olivér had secured the truck. The principal, a jovial man in his 50's, his black hair streaked with white, greeted us. He ushered all of us into the school cafeteria and sent his assistant for Andrea. He hadn't told her about the phone call from Mother.

When Andrea walked into the cafeteria, she froze, amazed to see all of us sitting there. Her eyes grew incredibly wide as she saw Father. Running to him, her arms flew around his waist, and her eyes filled with tears. Anikó, jumped down from Mother's lap and hurried over to her.

"Drea, Drea," she shouted with joy.

Of course, Andorina was quick to follow behind. She wrapped her arms around Andrea's legs, hugging her tightly.

The principal left quietly. Returning a few minutes later, he walked triumphantly behind a rolling cart with an enormous bowl of steaming stew. I sucked in my lower-lip to keep from drooling.

We enjoyed the hearty meal. The stew even had bits of meat in it. It was an incredible treat. During the four years that Dad was in prison, Mom could only afford to buy meat twice a month. And some weeks, when she had the money, the stores didn't have any in stock.

After the meal, Dad asked the principal how we could best get to Röjtök.

"I thought we were going to Ács," I said, totally surprised by the change in plans.

Father looked at me, annoyed that I had interrupted him. "András, there will be a lot of things that surprise you on this trip. Control that constant curiosity of yours, and don't interrupt me."

Filled with frustration, I picked up Andorina and put her on my lap.

"Really the best people to ask for directions would be the soldiers," the principal replied.

All of the adults stared at him in disbelief.

"Soldiers? You've got to be kidding?"

The principal smiled at Dad. "No, no. These are good Hungarian men from the village who were drafted into the Army against their will. Their loyalty is to the country and its people, not the Russian Communists."

"Are you sure they can be trusted?"

"Very sure," the principal said nodding. "Wait here, and I'll go get them." He stood and left immediately.

Father looked at Mr. Olivér, unsure of what to do.

"That's it then, he's going to have us arrested," Mr. Ródi said, running his hands through his thin brown hair. "Well it was worth a try, I suppose."

"Let's get out of here!" Mrs. Olivér's panicked voice filled the cafeteria as she frantically searched the faces of the others for agreement.

Andrea and I locked eyes. Our faces mirrored each other's fright.

"Don't upset the children," Mother said calmly. "I know the principal, not very well, but I think he can be trusted."

Dad rubbed his hand on his chin, "There's nothing we can do now, anyway."

Just then the principal, smiling broadly, stepped back into the cafeteria. Three soldiers followed him; a captain, a sergeant and a private. They were all dressed in long blue-gray Army coats and carried pistols on their wide belts.

"These men will help you," the principal said taking a seat.

One of the soldiers, the private, walked over to me without hesitation and picked Andorina up from my lap. I instantly turned my head toward Mother. She was half-way out of her seat desperately reaching for the twin when the private said, "I have a little girl just about her age. It's our first child!" he beamed proudly.

Mother eased back down without taking her eyes off of Andorina who, I noticed, was happily playing with the buttons on the private's coat.

"I hear you want to go to Röjtök." The captain addressed Father.

"Yes."

"Well, now, if I were going to take my lovely wife and children to Röjtök, I'd get me one of those fancy Russian limousines, filled with Russian caviar and vodka, and I'd have the maids and chef follow in a big American car, but you don't seem to want anyone to know you're taking a little trip," he said with a smile.

Dad and Mr. Olivér shook their heads and laughed. Mrs. Olivér didn't get it. She glared at the captain, her whole body tense.

"It's very kind of you to take your children on a field trip through our beautiful country, and as your tour guide, I'd recommend going through the city of Pápa on your way to Röjtök." The captain turned, "Sergeant, be kind enough to open that map you have in your pocket, you know the one, 'Best kept secrets about vacationing in Hungary'."

Mother laughed at his absurd statement.

"What's wrong with him?" Andrea asked in her logical fashion.

"Nothing. Not a thing," Mom replied smiling. "He knows exactly why we're here and what we want."

As Dad, the truck driver, Mr. Olivér and the captain planned our route, the private, still holding Andorina, spoke up, "You'll want to drive through the cities between here and Röjtök rather than around them."

"Excellent point young man. You'll make a good travel agent someday," commented the captain. "It's much too dangerous to try and drive around the cities. Although the cities are crawling with Communist soldiers, the Russians have check-points along all of the country roads. They'll be less suspicious of you if you drive right through the cities rather than around them. Besides, you wouldn't want to deprive your beautiful wives of the shopping they plan to do."

Dad and Mr. Olivér broke out laughing.

"Mother, this is ridiculous!" Andrea said, leaning toward her. "Here we are trying to do something very serious, and he keeps joking about it!"

"Calm down, Andrea." Mother patted her on the back. "It's good to hear your father laugh. The captain knows what he's doing. A little humor is a healthy way to deal with a difficult situation."

"Yeah, Andrea," I said leaning toward her, "laugh a little. Your face won't crack."

She stuck her tongue out at me. I was beginning to think that at thirteen, Andrea was quickly reaching the point of becoming a real bore.

The private handed Andorina back to me and walked over to the captain and sergeant.

"Well, my adventurous friends," said the captain as he stood up, "you'd better get your beauty sleep. With the road you must take, you will need six to seven hours to reach Röjtök tomorrow."

Shaking hands with Father, Mr. Olivér and the truck driver, the captain tipped his hat in the direction of Mom and Mrs. Olivér.

He turned to the principal. "Another meeting like this and you'll have made me an expert on field trips." With that the three soldiers smiled and left.

"Come, let me show you to your rooms. You must be very tired," the principal stated. Indicating for us to pick up our coats, he ushered us into the hallway. We walked down two dimly lit corridors. "Here, each family can have a room, and you three," he said pointing at the truck driver, Granddad and Mr. Ródi, "take number 112, two doors down. The bathroom is at the end of the hall. I'll have breakfast waiting for you at 5:30 a.m. in the cafeteria. You'll have to finish by 6:00 to avoid the students." He said 'goodnight' and left.

There were two beds in the small room. Dad sat down on the only chair and watched Mom help the twins off with their clothes. They were already half asleep.

Gazing at them struggling out of their clothes, Dad looked at Mother. "You know, Justine, I don't even know which is which," he said shaking his head.

Mom smiled up at him. "It's okay Kálmán, you haven't had time to get to know them yet. Once you do, it's fairly easy to tell them apart." She paused, tickling one of the twins, "this one is Anikó."

"My name is Anreen!" Andorina declared proudly pointing at herself.

Mother turned to Andrea, "Look in the closet please, and see if there are any extra blankets."

Andrea discovered a pile of blankets and pillows in the narrow closet.

"András, make a pallet for yourself. Andrea, you'll sleep in the bed with the twins."

I tossed the blankets down near the head of the two beds. Too tired to complain about my mother's decision

85

to give the bed to Andrea, I quickly stripped to my underwear and jumped under the covers to keep from freezing.

As everybody settled in and said 'goodnight', I suddenly remembered the one question that had been bothering me all evening. Looking through the darkness at Father, I began hesitantly, "Dad,...I know you told me not to ask any questions..."

Father sighed deeply.

"I only have one question, Dad," I rushed on, "would you please tell me why we're going to Röjtök?" I held my breath.

He didn't answer right away. "The reason," he began patiently, "is because it's very close to the border, about ten to twelve miles from Austria, and Mrs. Olivér has cousins in the village who can help us. We don't know anyone in Ács."

"Thanks, Dad," I replied and happily fell asleep. My dreams didn't warn me that I'd never see my Grandfather again.

CHAPTER TWELVE

LOSING GRANDFATHER

Dad awakened us at 5:00 the next morning. Marching the four of us down to the bathroom, he made sure we washed properly before going to the cafeteria for breakfast. Everyone from the truck was already there except Mother and Granddad.

Mom hurried in with a worried look on her face just seconds after we started eating. "Kálmán, I can't find Dad. I went to his room to make sure he was awake but he wasn't there. He's gone!"

Father stopped eating. "What do you mean he's gone? Did you check the bathroom?"

"Yes, Kálmán," Mom replied impatiently. "We have to find him. He gets confused and lost so easily!"

Dad, Mr. Olivér, the truck driver and Mr. Ródi stood immediately and hurried out the door.

Looking at us, Mom hesitated a moment. Facing Mrs. Olivér she asked, "Would you keep an eye on the children?" and ran after the men without waiting for a reply.

I yelled after her, "Mom!" and pushed away from the table.

"No András. Stay here," Mrs. Olivér said evenly, "They'll find him."

I stared at the door with frustration. "Where in the world could Granddad have gone? He doesn't even know this place!"

"He knows it a little. Remember, he's the one who brought me here," Andrea replied quietly.

We quickly finished eating. Mrs. Olivér took Píri and Árpád by the hand and told the rest of us to follow her back to her room.

The twins sat on the floor playing some sort of secret game with their hands. I'd never been able to understand what exactly they were doing, and whenever I asked Andorina she simply replied, "Twin game."

Píri and Andrea sat on one of the beds talking seriously about who knows what. I didn't care. Mrs. Olivér sat with her son close to her on the other bed in total silence.

I stared out the small window, feeling like a prisoner, praying they'd find Grandfather soon.

An entire hour passed before Mr. Olivér burst through the door, "Come on, get your coats. We're going."

Filled with hope, I looked up at Mr. Olivér.

"I'm sorry András, we didn't find him."

"We have to!" I yelled.

"We've looked everywhere. He's simply gone." He turned and left.

I couldn't believe it! I rushed out to the truck. Mother was talking to the principal.

"Thank you. I appreciate your help."

The principal nodded and walked away.

"Mom! We can't leave without Granddad!" I insisted.

She turned to me with tears in her eyes, "Where could he have gone?"

"I don't know, but we have to find him!" I jerked my head to the left, searching the school grounds frantically.

"András, we've lost precious time looking for him. It's already seven o'clock. We can't wait any longer, we have to think about everyone else." Mother's desperate voice sounded distant and hollow. "I've asked the principal to keep an eye out for Granddad. He may come back here."

"Okay, everybody up on the truck, and hurry," ordered Father.

Andrea climbed on wearily, her school backpack in her hand.

"András, we have to go. We can't change our plans now," Dad said, looking at me and pointing to the truck.

I climbed up and kneeled at the back of the truck as we drove off, willing Grandfather to be on the road so we could pick him up.

I never saw him.

The sky stayed a dull gray. It was freezing cold sitting in the back of the open truck. Everyone sat close together, huddled in Mrs. Olivér's bedspreads. Andorina was to my right and Mr. Ródi to my left. Next to Andorina was Mother, then Anikó, Andrea, Píri, Árpád, and Mr. and Mrs. Olivér. We didn't talk. Everyone except Mr. Olivér and I had his or her eyes closed. The twins were asleep. I could hear Anikó gently snoring. My eyes skimmed across the cold, drawn faces in the truck to the landscape surrounding us. The rows of rich, dark soil resting on the neatly plowed fields looked like endless cords of thick, black rope. Smooth, rolling hills snaked around us as if two large hands had gently placed mounds of soil on the land and tenderly sculpted and packed the dirt down. Clusters of tall, majestic trees were scattered like small forests between the vast, flat acres of naked fields and ran up the ridges of the round hills. Escaping had filled me with an almost unbearable sense of adventure, danger and triumph. Now, as I shivered under the blanket thinking of Grandfather, I felt a deep emptiness, uncertainty, and a penetrating sadness.

We drove west, toward Austria. It took us just over four hours to reach the small city of Pápa. As we entered the city, the cobblestone streets and the traffic awoke everyone on the truck. Tired and cold, no one spoke or even moved to catch a glimpse of the city.

Curious, I turned and peered through the window of the cab. Soldiers! They were everywhere! Military trucks rumbled down the streets and tanks sat like permanent fixtures at every intersection. I sat down fast and shot a quick glance at Mr. Olivér, whose eyes had been fixed toward the back of the truck. His round face was rosy from the cold. Scooting down, his head several inches below the sideboard, he whispered to me, "Pápa is important to the Russians. There's a relatively large military airport here."

I stared in disbelief. What were we doing driving right through a city with a Russian base? We were supposed to be escaping! People escape along back roads and alleys, in the middle of the night! Not smack through a city with thousands of soldiers! Numb with fright, I shut my eyes tightly waiting for a shot to ring out.

It felt like an hour but in reality it only took minutes before I noticed the city noise becoming distant. I immediately sat up on my knees. We were on a two-lane country road. I breathed deeply, trying to relieve the painful tightness in my chest. The danger of being stopped had passed.

Looking toward the back of the truck, all I saw were empty fields plowed under for the winter and bare trees as gray as the sky. The road was empty and, except for an occasional flock of birds, it was very quiet. I calmed down, letting my eyes move lazily over the landscape.

Suddenly, the truck driver slammed his foot hard on the brakes. Lurching forward, I threw my hands behind my head to keep from smashing against the truck. Scrambling back to my knees, I turned quickly to look through the cab. A soldier! One lousy soldier in the middle of nowhere! He stood perfectly still in the center of the road with a machine gun in his hands! Just a few feet behind him, to the side of the road, was an olive-green tent. The soldier didn't move. The truck stopped. Our driver left the engine running. Mother yanked on my coat, pointing for me to sit down. As I covered my legs with the bedspread, the tense silence in the truck hit me. I quickly scanned the faces surrounding me. Each cold, tired face was drawn, pale and terrified.

The soldier approached the cab. "Give me your papers!" he demanded. He was Hungarian but wore the uniform of the Russian military. Short and stocky, he appeared to have a powerful build under his thick military coat.

Father reached into his pocket and handed over the papers. Unfolding them, the soldier merely glanced at the papers and began to slowly walk around the truck. We didn't dare look at each other. Everyone stared into space or into their laps. No one moved. My mind was whirling. *How could we pass through a city teeming with thousands of soldiers and be stopped on an abandoned country road by one man in uniform? The machine gun is the only problem,* I decided. *With four men on the truck, the soldier is outnumbered. We could overpower him, and no one would know. Somebody just has to make the first move.* I hoped it would be Dad.

His face grim, the soldier took his time walking around the truck, craning his neck a bit to look at each of us. His eyes moved slowly over each child, counting. *We aren't supposed to be here, none of us. The papers are forged. We are traveling illegally. He has to know! There is no way he is going to believe we are on our way to Ács to rebuild a sugar factory, not with six kids who aren't old enough to work!* The soldier reached the driver's side of the truck, glanced into the cab and then began walking around the truck again! I couldn't believe it! There was nothing else to see! He moved slowly, leaning into the bed of the truck near the back. His eyes were hard and cold, his thin lips pressed together tightly. He rested the tip of his machine gun on the side of the truck. He was going to shoot us! I realized how easy it was going to be for him. We were sitting targets. Statues paralyzed by fear. All he had to do was move the gun a few inches, first to the left then the right.

He stepped back silently, moving the tip of his machine gun off of the truck. My heart pounded frantically. *What is he planning to do? He only has two choices, arrest us or shoot us!*

Reaching the passenger side of the truck the soldier turned to face Dad. Without a word, he handed the papers back through the window and stared at Father. Then, with the slightest nod of his head, he said, "God bless you."

"All right! Let's go!" I yelled before I even knew I had opened my mouth. The driver yanked the truck into gear and slowly pulled away from the soldier. Every adult in the back of the truck glared at me with shocked anger.

"Are you insane?" Mother hissed through clenched teeth.

"What?" I asked meekly.

"Never, ever open your mouth again!" she ordered severely.

I instantly clamped my lips together to show Mom I understood, but the relief I felt from yelling those few words radiated throughout my body.

We arrived near the border, in the tiny village of Röjtök, around 2:00 that afternoon. The driver stopped the truck in front of a gray, one-story house. As we climbed off the back of the truck, I saw each adult quickly pull the watch off his or her wrist and hand it to the driver. He left immediately.

We hurried into the house. Mrs. Olivér introduced us to her cousins who were sisters, Ilóna and Elizabeth. The women were in their early thirties. Both had light-brown hair. Ilóna was quite thin while Elizabeth was round, but not fat. They welcomed us with open arms. Elizabeth explained that their brother, Imre, was working and would be home around 5:00 p.m.

Sitting next to me, Dad said, "Imre will take us across. There are two small villages right on the border, Kövesd on the Hungarian side and an Austrian village right next to it. He'll explain how we can get across when he gets home tonight."

"Aren't there soldiers at the border?"

"Of course."

"Then how are we supposed to get across? Are we just going to walk across?" I asked, amazed at the simple plan.

"I don't know, András," Father said impatiently. "We'll have to wait for Imre."

I took my coat off. All eleven of us needed to use the one bathroom. I waited in line. I couldn't believe Dad didn't know how we were going to escape. I thought he and Mr. Olivér had planned every detail. How could they not know?

Everybody eventually settled in the small, but tidy living room. Mrs. Olivér excitedly began to tell her cousins about our trip from Budapest. Less than ten minutes after our arrival, we heard a knock on the front door. All of us were startled into silence. The sisters weren't expecting anyone. We stared at the door, frightened that someone had reported our arrival to the soldiers in the area. Ilóna rose, took a deep breath and slowly walked toward the door. Hesitantly grabbing the round knob, she opened it slowly. I saw a smile of relief spread across her face. Standing on the stoop was an old, squat woman with a small basket.

"I've brought a few eggs because I see you have guests."

"Thank you kindly, Mrs. Szabo." Ilóna responded, taking the offered basket gently. "Eggs!" she said holding one up for us to see.

Mr. Ródi laughed nervously, breaking the tension.

Ilóna headed toward the kitchen with the basket of eggs but soon returned carrying a tray full of teacakes and milk.

I was so hungry, I wanted to stuff everything on the tray into my mouth. None of us had had anything to eat since breakfast.

Another knock on the door interrupted us. Ilóna and Elizabeth exchanged glances. I quickly popped a teacake into my mouth and chewed rapidly.

Ilóna stood and went to the door. This time she opened it immediately, and I saw another bright smile. Turning toward us she said, "Canned tomatoes and squash! We'll have a proper meal for supper!"

By the time I heard the third knock on the door, the only question in my mind was *What was in the basket?* I was famished! In all, six women from the small village came to the door within two hours of our arrival. Each one carried a basket full of food. Their generosity was overwhelming.

Imre walked in the front door at 5:30 p.m. Taking a few steps toward the living room he stopped. I don't think he expected to see eleven people in his house. Elizabeth and Ilóna hurried in from the kitchen and quickly made introductions.

Imre had a kind face with eyes that sparkled. His black hair was very short and stood straight up on the top of his head.

The sisters went back to the kitchen to finish preparing supper. Imre removed his coat and went to sit next to Mr. and Mrs. Olivér. I desperately wanted to ask Imre how he planned to get us across the border. *Could we go tonight?*

Maybe we'd have to wait until tomorrow. How many soldiers were at the border? I waited impatiently.

Imre exchanged a few words about family with Mrs. Olivér. As their conversation slackened off, Mr. Olivér cleared his throat. "Imre, you must know why we're here. We want to escape into Austria."

"Of course, no problem," Imre replied, "but I can't take this many people across at the same time," gesturing with his arm at the room full of people. "We'll have to split you into two groups."

Mr. Olivér's eyes scanned the room quickly. "Well, that's fairly simple. Mr. and Mrs. Máday with their four children and the four of us with Mr. Ródi."

Imre shook his head. "We have to divide the children up more equally between the two groups. Four kids in one group will be too obvious to the border guards."

"Okay, we'll take one of the twins," Mrs. Olivér volunteered.

Mother was shocked. "No. They're too young. They must stay together. Andrea is the oldest. She'll go with you."

I immediately looked toward Andrea. She was silent but sat up stiffly at the mention of her name. I felt badly for her. Just yesterday she had been reunited with us, and now Mother was telling Andrea she'd have to leave the family again.

"All right, that'll have to work," Imre replied. "One more thing. I'd like Mr. Ródi to go with the second group. A third adult with those two young ones," he pointed at the twins, "will be very helpful."

Mr. Ródi nodded. He hadn't said more than a dozen words to anyone since we left Budapest. Mom told me yesterday that Mr. Ródi had been a councilman in Budapest. Like Father, he also was arrested as a political prisoner and spent five terrifying years in prison.

"Tomorrow's Saturday. We'll leave here with the first group around 10:00 in the morning." Imre continued, "A good friend of mine in the village will drive us in his cart to Kövesd. Now, there's really nothing but a railroad crossing bar between Kövesd and the Austrian village."

"Isn't it heavily guarded by soldiers?" interrupted Dad.

"Yes, of course, but I go there every other week. I know it well. You see, except for the crossing bar and border guards, the villages are so close together it looks like one town. And before the Communists outlawed traveling outside of Hungary, the people from the two villages came and went as they pleased. A lot of marriages have taken place between the people of the villages, so each village has relatives on the other side of the border."

Tense and excited, I leaned forward in my chair as Imre continued.

"The border guards...most of them are young, simple Hungarian men who were forced to join the army. I don't think we'll have much difficulty." Imre stopped a moment, thinking about what he had just said. Looking at him, I hoped he was right.

"The guards do keep a sharp lookout for anyone trying to escape, but every Saturday and Sunday, from noon until one o'clock, the relatives from the two villages are allowed to meet and talk across the border and exchange gifts or food or whatever. The area where they meet is very small

97

and usually there are so many people visiting that the soldiers can't keep track of everyone. I've often seen a young child run under the bar to hug his grandmother or uncle who lives in the Austrian village, and then the parents follow the child. Lots of people cross. The soldiers simply can't keep an eye on everyone!" Imre finished with a smile.

"It seems so easy," Mr. Olivér commented.

"It is," Imre replied.

It was a good plan, I thought. Anikó and Andorina could run under the bar and Mom and Dad would have to run after them. It would cause a commotion, and then Mr. Ródi and I would slip past the guards. We could even take a couple of the baskets some of the women had brought food in, fill them with rocks and cover them with a cloth, pretending they were gifts for relatives.

CHAPTER THIRTEEN

ARRESTED AT THE BORDER

Ilóna and Elizabeth made soft pallets for us to sleep on. People were sleeping everywhere in that small house!

Early the next morning I had to step carefully over five slumbering bodies to make the short trip to the bathroom. The door was locked. I waited impatiently feeling a growing excitement spread throughout my body. Today the Olivér family and Andrea would sneak across the border. We'd follow tomorrow. It dawned on me as I leaned against the wall, waiting, that exactly one month from today was Christmas Eve. This would be my very first Christmas in a free country! I smiled at the thought, yet the meaning of freedom, something Mother so desperately wanted, was difficult to imagine. I couldn't really understand it. All I knew was that we were going to live in a foreign country and that escaping was the biggest adventure of my life.

Andrea walked out of the bathroom. "I should have known it was you in there! Are you sure you don't need another hour to fix your hair? There's a few strands out of place!"

"You'd better hurry and empty your bladder, András. It's affecting your brain!"

I grinned, "Well at least I have a brain!"

"Oh yeah, well how do you think I make straight A's!" Andrea paused, then quickly added, "Never mind, don't answer that!"

We stood in silence for a moment, "Are you scared?" I asked in a hushed tone.

She nodded, looking down at her feet. "It sounds too easy!"

"After what we've been through...yeah, it does sound too easy, but Imre seems to know what he's doing." It was awkward talking about the escape.

"Listen Andrea, you're going across today. Tomorrow we'll follow, and in one month, it'll be Christmas!"

She looked at me with tears in her eyes. "I'm really scared! Not just about getting past the soldiers and escaping, but what's it going to be like over there? Where are we going to live?"

I put my hand in hers, "I don't know, but I think it'll be fun. Besides, think of all the food we'll have!"

Andrea frowned, "You're going to be a very fat man someday, András. Your stomach is going to be so big, you won't be able to see your feet! And your legs will be so fat, you won't be able to walk! Your..."

"Okay, okay! But it'll be a lot better than what we've had. I never want to eat boiled potatoes again!"

"All right, go on, get in there before your bladder explodes!"

I put my hand on the doorknob then turned to face Andrea, "Good luck today."

Andrea nodded nervously.

Ilóna and Elizabeth cooked a fabulous breakfast for us. The eggs the old woman had given us yesterday sat scrambled and steaming in the center of the table. I sat on my hands to keep from grabbing the entire plate for myself. The twins looked at the food wide-eyed. Mom had only been able to buy two or three eggs a month in Budapest. These she used for baking. The twins had never tasted scrambled eggs!

After breakfast, everyone, except Imre who had gone out early, waited expectantly in the living room. The six of us kids sat on the floor. The twins were playing their odd game again. No one spoke much. I looked up at the adults occasionally. Mom and Dad, sitting side-by-side, exchanged nervous glances. Mrs. Olivér, her dry hands clasped in her lap, would occasionally rub them together in a constant, fluid motion. Mr. Olivér stared at the front door. The quiet tension in the room hung over us like a dark, menacing cloud.

At 10:30 a.m. an old farmer, Mr. Bak, pulled up outside the house in a horse drawn cart. Imre jumped off and hurried into the house.

"Okay, come on," he indicated to the Olivérs and Andrea.

Mother pulled Andrea to her, whispered something and hugged her tightly. Andrea pushed away, her head hanging, and picked up her bookbag.

"No, leave that with us. We'll bring it tomorrow," Dad told her as he kissed her cheek.

"Hurry up!" Imre insisted.

The four Olivérs and Andrea climbed on the small cart and left. No one waved goodbye.

We waited. All day long we waited for Imre to come back. The longer we waited the more restless I felt. I thought I'd go crazy if I didn't get out of the house, even for just a few minutes. There was nothing to do. I went over to Father.

"Dad, can't I please go out? At least let me go in the backyard," I pleaded.

"No, András. You have to stay indoors. This is a small village. Everybody knows everyone who lives here. They'll know you're a stranger, and someone might report you to the local police or even the soldiers. We have to be careful!"

I turned away abruptly and went over to the stairs. Sitting on the bottom step, elbows on my knees and chin resting in my hands, I stared at the front door.

Imre arrived home at 4:00 p.m. The satisfying grin on his face when he walked in dissipated the thick cloud of anxiety which hung in the house. "They got across fine!"

Dad shook Imre's hand and slapped him on the back, "Were there any problems?"

"No. Getting them across wasn't a problem at all. It's too bad I didn't take all of you today! Everyone could have crossed easily. There were so many people at the border, the soldiers just gave up trying to keep track of who belonged to which side."

Mother was glowing with happiness. "Tomorrow, freedom!" she said as if making a toast. We congratulated Imre throughout the evening and anxiously anticipated our escape on Sunday.

Mr. Bak came for us at 10:00 a.m. Ilóna and Elizabeth said goodbye tearfully, wishing us a happy and long life, and told us to give the Olivér family their love when we caught up with them that afternoon. They told Imre they'd make an exceptional dinner for him when he returned home.

Dad and Mr. Ródi lifted the twins onto the cart and climbed up after them. Imre jumped up next to Mr. Bak. I sat at the head of the cart, just behind Imre. Dad sat across from me. Mother was next to him with Anikó snuggling between them. Andorina was by my side and Mr. Ródi next to her. We were off! The two horses plodded along slowly over the frozen dirt road. It was extremely cold. The light drizzle from the gray sky chilled me immediately. I pulled Andorina onto my lap and wrapped my arms around her.

Two hours later we arrived at the outskirts of the small village of Kövesd. The farm houses and barns were very old and definitely in need of repair and a fresh coat of paint. We reached the paved streets that led to the center of the village and approached the main square. As Mr. Bak gently urged his tired horses on, Dad sat up straight staring at the square.

"Imre, are you crazy!" he hissed.

I turned to look in the same direction as Dad and froze. Nausea rushed through my body. The small village square made of cobblestones and lined with large, tall trees was filled with Russian trucks and jeeps! Soldiers and civilians milled about. On one side of the square, farmers were selling vegetables and other goods from their handcrafted carts.

Across the square from the farmers was a long wooden table. A crowd of soldiers sat hunched together, stopping everyone entering the square.

"No problem, Kálmán," Imre said, turning slightly.

"Turn around and get out of here!"

Old Mr. Bak calmly turned the horses around not more than 15 yards from the table with the soldiers. They looked up at the cart, curiosity filling their faces, but none of them stood to stop us.

Safely away from the square, Imre turned toward us and shrugged, "They weren't there yesterday," he said apologetically.

Father closed his eyes and exhaled. Mom's face was as white as a sheet and Mr. Ródi looked sick. The twins were smiling at each other. I looked at the profile of Mr. Bak. His tanned, wrinkled face was calm but the ends of his white, handle-bar mustache twitched nervously. He and Imre decided to take us to another small village nearby.

We sat in silence. The hard-packed dirt road was lined with thin trees and bushes on either side. I didn't pay much attention to the few farmers and women we passed on the road. In the near distance, we saw a small forest.

"Look!" Mother exclaimed. Urging our eyes to follow her out-stretched arm, "The Austrian flag!"

Mr. Ródi and I sat up and stared. Just beyond the small forest, high on a pole, flew the red and white stripped Austrian flag.

"That's it. You can cross here," Imre said confidently.

Mr. Bak stopped the cart and spoke gently to his horses. I looked in the direction of the flag as Mom and Dad quickly lifted the twins from the cart. We'd have to walk about three hundred yards across the plowed field to make it to the small forest, then through the forest to Austria.

I jumped off the cart ready to walk when Dad and Mother, each holding the hand of one of the twins, began running across the plowed field. Imre was running with them and Mr. Ródi was right behind. Stunned for a second, I took off, quickly catching up with Mom and Andorina. I grabbed Andorina's empty hand, helping her along. Suddenly shots rang out! I was about to stop but Mom just kept running. Frantically, I scanned the forest. I couldn't tell where the shots came from. More shots were fired. The blast from the rifles rang in my ears. Someone was yelling. I panicked and let go of Andorina's hand. Mom didn't stop. She was running hard. Running toward her dream.

Dad shouted, "Stop!"

Mother looked toward him and stopped immediately, her eyes filled with desperation.

Breathing heavily, Father said, "The bullets are too close. The next round will hit us."

We stood as still as statues just 50 yards from the forest and watched two soldiers, rifles raised, march toward us. I looked at them in disbelief. We were so close! And these two soldiers were all that stood in our way. They couldn't have been more than 18 or 19 years old! One of them pointed his gun at Father, told him to turn around and head back to the road. We turned reluctantly, silently, away from the small forest.

The cart was gone. We reached the road and stood close together. Dad looked at the young soldiers who seemed to be at a loss as to what to do next.

"Are you from around here?" Dad asked pleasantly.

"Yes, I was born in Lövö," replied the young blond soldier.

"I live in the next village," the other, stocky and dark, responded as if answering a simple questionnaire.

"You're good soldiers, I can see that," Imre told them confidently. "I live in Röjtök."

"I know where that is," the stocky soldier said.

"We're all just simple farmers," Imre continued smoothly. "Good Hungarians who work hard to plow the fields and bring in the crops. You don't want to hand your neighbors over to the Russians."

The slim blond soldier looked hard at Imre. "You were trying to escape. It's our duty to capture escapees. What the Russians do with you afterwards is no concern of ours."

Mr. Ródi spoke up, surprising everyone. Stepping directly in front of the soldiers he looked from one to the other. "You've never been imprisoned and tortured by the Russians, have you? They beat me until I was black and blue all over. Not one inch of my body resembled a human being. Those black boots you're wearing kicked me until I was unconscious and then kicked me again! They tore out my fingernails, slowly, one-by-one, and crushed their lighted cigarettes on my legs. They murdered my wife and brother!" His eyes were filled with hatred. "What kind of Hungarians are you to hand a mother and her children over to such animals!"

The soldiers stepped back in astonishment. "Look," the stocky one began, "we're the border patrol here. We can't let you cross. This morning our Communist commander told us we'd be shot if we allowed anyone to escape."

"Okay, we don't want to get you in trouble," Father said calmly. "Just let us go. We'll walk to the next village and disappear."

"We won't try to cross the border," Imre added.

Mr. Ródi nodded his head. "You must think of the children," he said pointing at the twins and me. "They are much too young to understand what is happening. Think of the little children in your own village."

Shoulders sagging, the young men looked at each other. Mr. Ródi's eyes were filled with hope.

"Come on, we'll just start down the road. Stay here and watch us if you like," Imre urged them.

I looked up at Mother, ready to walk away quickly. My feet were numb from the cold, and the twins were growing restless.

The soldiers stepped away from us, speaking in hushed tones.

The blond one turned back toward us. They were going to let us go!

Suddenly he jerked his head toward the road. We immediately turned to look in the same direction. A large Russian military truck stopped in the middle of the road a fair distance from us. Three soldiers jumped off, pulled large wooden signs nailed onto stakes from inside of the truck and pounded them into the ground.

I quickly looked at the two soldiers standing with us. Faces white as ghosts, their eyes were filled with fear. The truck began moving toward us, stopped a short distance from where we stood and the soldiers hammered more stakes into the frozen ground by the side of the road.

The truck started up again. I breathed in sharply knowing they'd pick us up. But they didn't! The truck passed right by us! I couldn't believe it! The driver glanced our way when the truck was parallel to us but kept on going. I ran the short distance down the road where they had pounded the signs into the frozen ground. "Warning! Mine Fields!"

I turned in the direction of the small forest. The sign said it was mined! But we didn't step on any mines! And there were seven of us running all over that field!

"András, come here!" Father yelled harshly.

I ran back to the group just as the blond soldier cleared his throat and started talking. He looked terrified. "That's it! We're turning you in!" he said with a finality that left no room for argument.

My mind screamed, *No!* I looked at the soldiers with a hatred I'd never known. Another minute, and they would have let us go! I stared at the stupid Russian truck moving slowly down the road. If only the soldiers had given us permission to leave!

The blond soldier told his comrade to keep his rifle pointed at us while he went into the village to report our capture. Father stood next to Mom and put his arm around her. Mr. Ródi stood absolutely still, staring toward the forest. Imre looked at the soldier guarding us and decided it was useless to talk to him. The soldier gripped his rifle so hard his knuckles were white.

A small military truck rumbled down the road toward us 20 minutes later. It was well past three o'clock. We were ordered onto the truck at gun point and driven a short distance to a border patrol station; a small house used by the guards. The soldiers escorted us into an office furnished with one desk and four chairs. The tiny window behind the desk had thick bars on the outside. Told to wait for the second-lieutenant, Mother turned to Dad, "What are we going to say when they question us?"

Father thought for a moment. "We have to protect the children. I'll tell them I wanted to escape. You tell them you didn't want to leave Hungary, that I forced you and the kids to go with me. That way they might let you go back to Budapest."

Mother nodded dejectedly. Imre leaned against a wall, scratching his chin nervously. Mr. Ródi sat with his head bowed.

Thirty minutes later, the second-lieutenant, a short, clean-shaven man, marched into the office. The first thing I noticed was his black uniform and the colors on his jacket collar, they were blood red! He was a member of the secret police!

Taking us in with a quick glance, he walked behind the desk, "Empty your pockets! Everybody! The little ones too!" he said harshly pointing at the twins.

Identification cards, kleenex, money, forged travel papers, a small pocket knife and the books from Andrea's school bag littered the desk.

Looking at each item, the second-lieutenant slipped the small pocket knife into his jacket. He picked up the identification cards and travel papers studying each one carefully. Occasionally he looked up at one of us but didn't say a word. We stood in total silence barely daring to breathe.

The second-lieutenant tossed the papers on the desk with disgust and glared at us. "Tomorrow morning you will be taken away." With that he rose and walked out of the room, locking the door behind him.

Imre sighed and scratched his head. Mom looked at Dad, shrugging her shoulders slightly. Everyone slowly approached the desk and returned their few belongings to their pockets.

"Aren't they going to feed us?" I asked, stunned.

"No. We're prisoners," Dad answered with an edge in his voice.

"Come on girls, let's make ourselves comfortable," Mom said to the twins, taking each by the hand. She looked around the small office in frustration. Choosing a corner of the room behind the desk, Mom sat down on the cold floor with a twin on either side of her.

"Now, lean close to me and go to sleep." Mother put an arm around each of them and closed her eyes.

"We're sleeping here?" I whispered to Dad.

"Yes! Get on the desk and lie down. Use Andrea's backpack as a pillow."

Reluctantly, I climbed onto the desk. Imre slumped against the wall by the door and slid to the floor. Mr. Ródi pulled an empty chair to him and propped his feet on it. Dad turned the light out and sat down.

I couldn't sleep. No one could. And no one could answer the questions that kept pounding in my head.

CHAPTER FOURTEEN

PRISONERS

A loud knock on the door startled us. It was early morning. My body ached all over as I sat up. Hungry and tired, I looked toward the door, anticipating food.

A soldier opened it, his hands empty. "Come on, let's go!" he ordered, indicating that we should follow him. We walked out into the freezing morning air. A military truck with a canvas cover was waiting for us. An officer and private stood near the back of the truck. Looking at Mom and the twins, the officer said, "You and the girls sit up front in the cab. The rest of you get in the back."

I climbed up quickly and sat down on the wooden bench bolted to the truck-bed. The private tied the canvas at the back of the truck, got into the cab and started the engine.

We drove for hours, stopping on occasion but were never allowed out of the truck. At every stop, the officer got out and spoke with someone. I could only catch a few meaningless words of the muted conversations. Dad, Imre and Mr. Ródi, their bodies slumped in resignation, sat far apart in total silence. I felt like an outcast in the back of the cold, dank truck. Looking at Dad, I realized there was an enormous void between us. I desperately wanted to slide next to Dad, have him put a strong, comforting arm around my shoulder and allow me to weep quietly. But after not seeing him for four years, he was still a stranger to me and I to him.

Near noon, we stopped again. Both doors of the cab slammed shut, and I heard the twins talking. The private untied the canvas cover and pulled it back.

"Szombathely," Dad whispered in my ear as we climbed down from the truck. This large city, just ten miles from the Hungarian-Austrian border, was quite a bit south of where we'd been arrested.

I quickly looked around. We were standing in front of a dull gray building, five stories high, with "Military Barracks" written above the entrance.

The barracks stood near the center of the city on a large square. Across the way were the main train station, shops and office buildings. As I turned toward the train station, a strong hand clamped down on my shoulder. It felt like an iron claw was sinking into my flesh. I jerked around to face the private. "Stop sight-seeing and get going!" he yelled, shoving me toward the wide steps of the barracks.

Inside, the center of the building was square and open, reaching all the way up to the fifth floor. Open walkways, protected by strong iron railings, ran the length of the walls. Wide, imposing stairs leading up to the first landing stood like stacked piano keys against the far wall. On each floor along the walkways, soldiers stood at attention next to heavy wooden doors. Some were closed, some open. The seven of us were escorted to the second floor. As we reached the landing, one of our guards hit Imre in the back with the butt of his rifle.

"You, go to the end of hall there and turn facing the wall!" Imre stumbled quickly toward the wall.

The rest of us were led into a very large room with high windows and a few chairs. The twins immediately

112

climbed onto two of the chairs and rhythmically began swinging their legs. Mother sat down next to them.

"Dad?" I asked hesitantly, "What do you think they'll do to us?"

Facing the closed door, he quietly answered, "I don't know."

I looked at Mr. Ródi, hoping to get more of a response, but he just stared at the floor as if hypnotized.

"Dad, do you think they might give us something to eat?" I asked meekly.

He looked up at me with a slight smile and shook his head. "I don't know that either, András. I know you're hungry, we all are."

Twenty minutes passed. I waited for something to happen. Anything. No one spoke.

Three soldiers suddenly burst into the room. Each had pistols on their belts. "Come, follow us. It's time to eat."

I immediately jumped up and grinned at Dad. He looked at me with such anger that I stopped instantly.

Grabbing me hard by the arm he hissed, "We're not going to a feast at Grandmother's! Remember, you're a prisoner!"

My mind reeled as he let go of me. I lost my appetite before I stepped out of the room.

The three soldiers, one in front and two behind us, led us to the stairs. I noticed that Imre was still standing facing the wall. We walked to the ground floor and were herded into a huge room filled with wooden tables and benches, and people! There were at least 75 people already eating at the tables. One of the soldiers pointed at an empty table. We sat down in front of chipped soup bowls, a plate of sliced bread, a pitcher of water and a large bowl of watery cabbage soup.

I leaned forward and looked around the room. Armed soldiers were stationed against all four walls. The only sound was the clinking of spoons against bowls. The other prisoners sat with heads hanging and drooped shoulders. Every face I caught a glimpse of looked either depressed or terrified.

The bread was stale, and the soup was terrible, but at least it was warm. We ate quickly. As soon as we finished, we were escorted back upstairs to the same room on the second floor. The twins, revitalized by the food, began running around in circles. Mother stood to stop them and then decided against it. Mr. Ródi paced slowly up and down along one side of the room. Mom and Dad sat close together, their heads almost touching and spoke in hushed tones. I leaned against the wall, my stomach still empty and aching. Looking up at the windows, I realized if I stood on a chair I could see out.

Quietly, I grabbed the sturdiest chair I could find and stepped up. Looking down onto the front yard of the barracks, I saw several prisoners from the dining room being loaded onto trucks.

"András!" Dad shouted.

Startled, I jumped down immediately.

"Is there anything your curiosity won't stop you from doing! You're a prisoner! Act like one!"

Mother smiled spontaneously. "Kálmán, how is he supposed to know how a prisoner should act?"

Dad spun around to face her. He looked so angry I thought he was going to hit her! Then I saw his shoulders sag and his entire body relax.

"You're right, Justine." Turning toward me he said, "András, pull that chair away from the window and come over here." I hurriedly obeyed him.

"Listen to me carefully," Dad began, his face just inches from mine. "A prisoner does everything he is told and nothing more, nothing less. We were told to wait here. That's what we do, wait. When you want to do something like stand on a chair to look out the window, you have to ask yourself if you were told to do it. Were you?"

I shook my head rapidly.

"And you weren't told not to do it." He looked at me hard.

I felt confused. *If the soldiers didn't tell me I couldn't look out the window, why was it wrong?*

"These soldiers have rules, special rules for prisoners, and the only time you find out if you've done something wrong is after you've done it. And the way you find out is by getting a beating."

I nodded, not daring to move. Vivid pictures flashed through my mind of Dad in prison being beaten and kicked and not knowing why.

"Go sit down," ordered Dad. I turned and quickly walked to a chair.

A soldier slammed the door open and announced, "We're taking you for interrogation!" He looked around and pointed at Mother. "You, you're first!"

"Can I bring my babies? They'll be quiet, I promise."

Looking at the twins, the soldier smirked, "No!"

In an instant I understood what Mom was trying to do. She wanted to take the twins to try and gain some sympathy from the interrogator.

"You!" The soldier yelled in my direction. "You come too! You're old enough to understand but perhaps too stupid to lie!"

I froze and looked at Mother. She stood up slowly. I walked stiffly to her side and followed the soldier out of the room.

We were escorted to the first floor, into an office with three desks. In front of each desk sat two chairs and behind each desk sat a man in a black uniform. I felt Mother tremble as we sat down to face the Secret Police.

"Your name!" He began immediately. The man had a long, bent nose and bushy black eyebrows above piercing black eyes. His chin was square and powerful. He was writing Mom's answers on a sheet of white paper. I noticed that his fingernails were manicured.

"Your address!" "Your age!" "Who is your father!" He spit the questions out like bullets.

Mother answered with a weak voice and began crying.

"I didn't want to leave, sir! I didn't want to leave my home, my country! I have two little babies! Why would I jeopardize their lives by trying to leave? I have a father

116

in Budapest who is old and sick. He needs me! I never wanted to leave! I want to go back to my poor, sick father."

I looked in shock at Mother. How could she break down in front of this horrible man! And then I remembered the conversation she and Dad had the night before at the border patrol station. She was supposed to do this! The Secret Policeman didn't look convinced.

"It's true," I added quickly, "Mom didn't want to go!"

The man leaned across the desk and grabbed my jacket, almost jerking me off of the chair.

"Did I ask you a question?"

"No!" I replied, shouting in his face.

"Then shut up!" he yelled back, pushing me hard into my seat.

Just then Father was brought into the small office and ushered to the desk on my right. I could hear him being asked the same questions as Mom. The man interrogating him was large and powerful. He had a neatly trimmed mustache which he stroked constantly with his forefinger.

Mother kept crying and pleading to be allowed to return to Budapest.

"You were trying to escape! You left the city without permission! That is a crime against the State!"

Mom just went on crying, but I could tell she was listening to the questions Dad was being asked.

"I'm a simple housewife with little children and a sick father. I never wanted to leave!" she cried, wiping the tears with her hand.

"Have you ever been convicted of a crime?" I heard the dreaded question directed at Dad. Father didn't answer.

Mother stole a glance at him, and her entire body tensed. She quickly covered her face with her hands, weeping silently.

I stared at the edge of the desk willing Father to answer the question. But how? If he told them he spent four years in prison they'd immediately take him away and shoot him!

Dad still didn't respond.

I sat on my hands and grasped the edge of the chair so hard my fingers screamed with pain. *Come on, Dad, say something!* I pleaded silently. If he didn't answer the question immediately, they'd know! The longer Dad kept quiet, the more suspicious they'd become.

It seemed like minutes before Father looked the Secret Policeman directly in the eye and said, "No."

No! my mind screamed! *They'll find out he has a prison record! It can't be that difficult to check! Surely the Communists have a list of all of the political prisoners who were freed in October! One phone call is all it'll take!*

Filled with dread, I waited for the interrogator to pick up the phone and make his call. He didn't do anything for a while. Gazing steadily at Dad for a full minute, he finally dropped his eyes and made a note on the sheet of paper in front of him.

I don't know how much longer we sat there. I felt so tired! The voices around me sounded distant and muffled.

Mother nudged me. She and Dad were standing. I slid out of the chair and followed. They took us back to the room on the second floor. Imre was still standing, facing the·wall. He hadn't moved in four hours.

They took Mr. Ródi for interrogation. He returned 30 minutes later. Exchanging glances, he and Dad passed a silent message. Two men whose past experience as prisoners required no words to communicate.

Father stood, opened the door and summoned the soldier guarding us.

"What's going to happen to us? It's almost four o'clock. Where are the others we saw in the dining room?" he asked the young soldier nervously.

"Oh, well, all of those prisoners were interrogated and then released." His voice was soft and friendly.

"Released?" Dad's eyebrows shot up.

"Yeah."

My heart jumped! If they let all of those people go... Then I remembered, "What about the people who were getting into the trucks?"

"Oh them, well see, those folk live in Budapest. We drove them there."

Father tensed. "We live there. Why weren't we taken with them?"

"Well, 'cause see, you're going to be turned over to the Russians."

The blood drained from Father's face. The soldier looked at him quizzically and left the room.

"Kálmán!" Mother's panicked voice was barely above a whisper.

Mr. Ródi began trembling uncontrollably. Dad's eyes searched the room erratically, looking for a way out.

"If they give us to the Russians, we'll end up in a labor camp...that's if we survive the trip." Mr. Ródi said as he fought to control the tears running down his pale cheeks.

"We've got to do something!" Dad said hoarsely.

"They let everybody else go! Why us?" I shouted totally panicked.

"It doesn't matter why! They've made their decision!" Mr. Ródi replied, terrified.

"Oh no!" Mother cried. She rushed over to Dad and quietly whispered, "The night before we left Budapest, I wrote down the names and addresses of all of the people we know in foreign countries! I sewed the paper under the lining of Anikó's coat."

"You have to get rid of it!" Father said urgently.

"Yes, yes of course."

"Justine, get the twins, put their coats on and take them to the bathroom. Tear the paper up and flush it down the toilet."

Mother nodded and carried out the task, returning with a grim look on her face. Helping the twins take off their coats, she sat dejectedly.

"We have to think of some way to get out of here!" Dad said to no one in particular as he paced up and down, running his hands through his thick, brown hair.

Mr. Ródi looked at him, "We'd better come up with something soon. They may come for us any minute."

I was in a frenzy. My eyes darted from Dad to Mr. Ródi to Mom and back to Dad. "Dad!" I yelled, losing control. "What are we going to do!"

Father stopped pacing. "Shut up, András, and let me think..." He stared at me oddly then looked over at Mom.

"Obnoxious noise. We'll make unbearable noise." He whispered his idea. Mom and Dad looked at me.

"András, come here quickly!" Dad ordered. Grabbing my shoulders with his strong hands he looked me in the eyes. "Listen carefully. I want you to start crying and yelling. Complain about being hungry and locked up in the room. Your Mother and I are going to tell you to stop but no matter how much we yell at you to stop, don't stop. I'll threaten to punish you. Ignore it. Don't stop crying until I say a password..."

"Tudo," Mother suggested immediately.

"Yes, that's good," Dad said turning toward her. "It doesn't mean anything, so there's no chance of someone else saying it."

He looked at me with urgency, "When I say, 'Tudo', you can stop crying. Until I do, keep making as much noise as you can no matter what anyone says. Understand?"

I nodded my head vigorously and took a deep breath.

"Now!" Father hissed.

I let out a piercing scream. Tears streamed down my face. The twins looked at me with startled expressions. Andorina's eyes welled up with tears, her jaw dropped and a powerful cry burst from her throat. Anikó immediately joined in. Our screams echoed in the empty room.

A soldier slammed open the door. Mom and Dad hurried to the twins, pretending to calm them. Mr. Ródi stood sternly in front of me.

"What's going on here! What's the problem?" demanded the soldier.

Mother looked up at him with a worried expression and innocently said, "I don't know."

He stood in the doorway for a moment, then left shutting the door behind him.

I kept crying and screaming. The twins, their eyes red and spilling tears, were really wailing.

A second soldier burst into the room. "What's the problem!" he yelled. Mom, Dad and Mr. Ródi rushed from child to child, telling us to be quiet. Mother again turned and said, "I don't know."

The soldier walked out quickly. A sergeant entered the room a few minutes later. Mom, Dad and Mr. Ródi were still rushing around trying to calm us.

"Just what is the problem here? Can't you make them stop crying? We can hear them all over the building! They're making too much noise!"

Father was yelling at me, threatening to punish me severely if I didn't stop screaming. I ignored him completely.

By now Mother had started to cry. She looked at the sergeant and frantically said, "I don't know! The children can't stand being locked up in this room anymore. It's terrible! They're hungry and tired! I want to go home!"

The Sergeant shook his head. I managed an ear-splitting scream just as he reached the door.

I cried harder. I knew this was the only chance we had of avoiding being handed over to the Russians. It had to work!

The Sergeant returned five minutes later looking extremely upset. Our cries grew louder. He stared at the six of us, shook his head and looked up at the ceiling. "You're too noisy! Get out of here! Go home!" he said as if surrendering to us.

"Tudo," Dad said quickly.

I stopped crying and wiped the tears from my eyes. The twins, still wailing, looked at me and slowly toned their cries down to whimpers.

Father, Mother and Mr. Ródi scrambled for our coats. This was it! We had to get out of there fast! I grabbed my coat, cap and Andrea's backpack. Mom and Dad rushed to dress the twins.

"Do you know where Imre is?" Dad asked them, his fingers rapidly buttoning Anikó's coat.

"He's in the hall," they said in unison.

"That's right. When we walk out of this room, I want you two to be proper little girls and go to him and tell him goodbye, okay?"

They nodded, their cheeks flushed from crying.

"We have very little time, so you must run over to Imre quickly, okay?"

"Okay Daddy," Anikó replied as he tied the scarf under her chin.

I couldn't understand what Father was doing! Surely we'd get in trouble for this. The twins didn't really know Imre. Why did Dad want them to say 'goodbye' to him? It was a waste of precious time!

We stepped out of the room and the twins took off down the hall toward Imre. I chased after them with Mom and Mr. Ródi close behind. Dad hurried after us but he didn't run. Mom, in a voice that sounded like she could care less, called out, "Girls, stop. Come back here." Mr. Ródi also said to stop, but he sounded like he was reading from a menu.

The soldier who was standing outside of our room yelled furiously. "Don't let the kids run over there!"

I stopped a few yards from Imre, but the twins kept running. Father immediately ran toward the twins just as they reached Imre. He turned away from the wall, looked down at the twins and said, "Hello!" He looked quickly at Father, who had just reached the girls and was lifting them up, one in each arm.

"Lövő. Dr. Geiger," Imre whispered hastily.

"You shouldn't have done that!" Dad began scolding the girls as he hurried back down the hall. "When the soldier tells you to do something, do it!" Dad went on and on, scolding them as we quickly headed for the stairs. The soldiers standing in the hallways followed us with their eyes. I wanted to take the stairs two at a time and run out of the building yelling with joy. I felt triumphant!

We hurried through the gate of the barracks and headed across the square toward the train station. The clock above the entrance to the station showed 4:30 p.m. Mr. Ródi suddenly stopped in the middle of the square and looked down at his feet.

"I can't take this anymore, Kálmán." he said quietly. "I have a terrible stomach ulcer." He looked up at Dad. "I didn't tell you this before, but I tried to escape earlier... a few weeks ago, on the 14th. When I was running across the fields toward the Austrian border my ulcer started bleeding badly. I collapsed. The pain was terrible. That's where the border patrol found me the next day. Lying on the ground, bleeding inside. I was arrested but too weak to be interrogated. They put me in a hospital with guards. I escaped from the hospital a week later." Mr. Ródi closed his eyes. "I can't do it again. I can't go on."

Dad reached out, gently patting Mr. Ródi's arm.

"If you don't want to come with us, then don't," he said quietly.

Mr. Ródi, tears in his eyes, nodded. "Goodbye and good luck." He turned and walked away.

CHAPTER FIFTEEN

THE KINDNESS OF STRANGERS

We hurried toward the train station. It was an enormous building with tall arches and thick columns. A cluster of ticket booths sat in the center of the lobby. Two wide corridors led to the tracks on either side of the booths. At the entrance to each corridor stood the train schedules listing arrivals and departures. The lobby was teeming with people. Some waited impatiently at the ticket booths, others hurried toward the rumbling trains. We made our way through the crowd to the schedule board.

"Quickly, help me find the next train for Lövő," Dad said, scanning the large board.

Our eyes desperately searched the schedule for departing trains.

"There it is!" Mother exclaimed. "The next train for Lövő is leaving at 5:00 p.m."

I looked around frantically for a clock and found one above the ticket booths. It was 4:50! We hurried toward the booths. The lines were long with farmers and laborers who lived in the many small villages in the surrounding countryside. Mother grabbed Anikó and quickly stood in a line. Dad, Andorina and I stood in another line, hoping one of us would get to a counter before 5:00. I stared at the clock nervously. The lines were moving so slowly! Eight people stood in front of us; seven in front of Mom and Anikó. I stomped my feet impatiently. Mom and Dad exchanged tense glances. I looked at the clock again. It was five minutes to five! Standing on my toes, I peered

126

past the line of people in front of me, trying to see what was taking so incredibly long. I tried not to look at the clock, hoping if I ignored it, time would stand still. But I couldn't stop my head from jerking up. It was three minutes before five! I wanted to scream at the people standing in front of me, at the ticket sellers, at the clock!

Dad grabbed Andorina and yelled, "Come on!"

Mom swept Anikó up into her arms and we broke into a run toward the corridor to our right. Five trains stood on the tracks. People were everywhere! My eyes desperately searched the waiting trains.

"There it is!" Dad shouted pointing at the train on the third track. "Hurry up!"

"We don't have tickets!" Mom whispered, trying to catch her breath as we ran toward the train.

"It doesn't matter. Get on!" Dad shoved us toward the steps. People were staring. We rushed onto the train as it started its slow, grinding escape from the station.

As the train lurched forward, we entered the passenger car hesitantly. It was full of farmers who had travelled to Sombathely to work or sell their goods. Moving down the aisle slowly, I glanced at the faces of the people seated on either side. Tired young men dressed in blue work slacks and coats, and old, wrinkled women with scarfs on their heads and thick socks under their long skirts. Their empty baskets and canvas bags were tucked safely above their heads in the luggage racks. I heard occasional whispered comments about the twins as we slowly made our way down the aisle. We found seats near the back of the car and quickly sat down, not daring to speak. I watched darkness

127

grow around us as we swayed to the rhythmic sound of the tracks.

The train made several stops at small villages. People got on and off, talking as they came and went about what they had sold and waving to each other as the train pulled out of the dark stations.

Mom and Dad sat in tense silence. I knew they were very worried about not having tickets. We could be arrested or at the very least thrown off the train at the next stop with nowhere to go.

"Good evening, everyone." The conductor closed the door behind him as he stepped into the car. Dad jumped, his body stiff with fear. The conductor slowly made his way down the aisle, punching tickets and exchanging a few words with the other passengers. He was at least six feet tall and round like a sturdy tree trunk.

"What if he works for the secret police or the Russians?" I whispered to Dad. My stomach tightened and the palms of my hands grew wet as the conductor came nearer.

"There's nothing we can do, son," he replied tensely.

The conductor reached our seats and grinned. "Oh, you folks are from the city!" he declared for all to hear.

Mother looked up, astonished and scared.

"Where do you want to go?" he asked matter-of-factly.

"Well," Father began tentatively, "we'd like to get off at Lövő. Would you please let us know when we reach the station?"

"Lövő? Sure." With that he turned and lumbered down the aisle without ever asking for our tickets.

Dad sighed and looked tensely at Mom. "It's out of our hands now, Justine. All we can do is wait."

Dad turned his head toward the window and stared at the black night. I slumped in my seat and closed my eyes. *Our only plan was the quickly whispered words by Imre. Find Dr. Geiger in Lövő. A total stranger. That's if we ever make it there!* I felt lost and surrendered my mind to questions it begged to have answered. *Where was Andrea? Where was Grandpa? What was Mr. Ródi going to do? And what would happen to Imre?*

I crossed my arms over my stomach. It was close to seven o'clock. Two hours on this slow train, and we hadn't eaten since noon. That foul cabbage soup we had at the barracks was beginning to appeal to my empty stomach.

The round conductor stepped into our car and hurried over.

"The next stop is Lövő. It'll be just a few minutes now."

"Thank you," Dad responded. "Could you tell me where a Dr. Geiger lives?"

The conductor grinned slightly. "I'll take care of that at the station," he replied, tipped his hat and left.

Mom and Dad put their coats on and helped the sleepy twins into theirs. I slipped my coat on and grabbed the backpack. When the train stopped, I thought they must have made a mistake. The small station was pitch black. It had to be the wrong stop. There couldn't be a village anywhere near this lifeless station.

Mom and Dad stepped off the train, each stooping quickly to lift a twin. Jumping to the platform, I blinked my eyes rapidly, trying to adjust to the darkness. The dim light from the cars splashed onto the concrete slab beneath our feet. I saw the conductor walking in our direction, greeting the other passengers as they got off. He approached a young woman standing close to us. "Mária, these folks are from Budapest. They want to go to Dr. Geiger's. Please show them the way."

"Sure," she responded cheerfully. She was holding the hand of a young girl at her side. I couldn't see either of their faces clearly.

"Come," Mária told us and started walking into the black night. As we followed her, the train pulled out, taking with it the only source of light. It was pitch black as we walked along the unfamiliar street. Mom and Dad each carried a twin.

"Hi Mária. Hi Kati." I jumped with fright. Mom and Dad froze.

"Hi Sándor," they called out as the dark figure of a young man passed us. I hadn't seen or heard that man approaching us. He stepped out of the darkness like a ghost.

Mária and little Kati walked on. I sucked in the cold night air, willing my racing heart to slow down. Dad motioned for me to follow quickly. We walked in silence for perhaps ten minutes before reaching the small village square. Dull lamps from the houses surrounding the square formed murky pools of light around the windows.

Mária stopped and pointed to a two story house. "That's where Dr. Geiger lives."

"Thank you very much," Father said and cautiously started toward the house. A low wood fence with an iron gate surrounded the small front yard. Father knocked on the fence, not daring to step inside the gate.

A stocky woman opened the front door, "Who's there?"

"My name is Kálmán Máday. Imre sent us."

She came toward us quickly, "Hurry, get inside!" She ushered us into the warm kitchen and called out for her husband.

Dr. Geiger came immediately, his long, white hair sticking out on both sides of his head. Father quickly explained to the doctor and his wife that Imre had given us the doctor's name and briefly told them about our attempted escape and capture.

Dr. Geiger nodded his head. "It's too late to cross the border tonight, young man. I'll turn the heat on in the attic. You and your family can sleep there tonight. We'll see what we can do for you in the morning."

Suddenly a knock jerked our heads toward the front door. Dr. Geiger looked at his terrified wife. He stood quickly, smoothed back his unruly white hair and answered the door. An old farmer entered grandly, greeting Dr. Geiger and his wife in a loud, arrogant voice. He stood with feet apart, swaying slightly and with a booming voice announced, "Come on, get on my cart. I'll take you!" Slender and short, he was powerfully built. He was also drunk.

"János, who told you we had guests!" Mrs. Geiger demanded.

He glared at her then smiled shyly, "I saw them," he began, pointing at us, "leave the train. They's city folk

131

sure as I'm country. Fresh air and cow manure is not what they came for."

Mom and Dad looked at each other, agreeing in an instant that this was not a man they could trust.

"Thanks, but I think we'll wait," Dad said kindly.

"What do you mean? You don't think I can gets across?"

"Maybe you can, but the children are tired. We'll wait until morning."

"Who do you think you are? You come here from the city and think you know better! I can get across the border anytime I feel like it! Those guards don't know nothin'. Get your coats and let's go!" He looked angry and indignant.

Dr. Geiger sighed and shook his head. His wife propped both of her arms on her hips. "János, you're in need of sleep, not some night-time adventure."

"An honorable Hungarian is always ready for adventure!" he replied to her, then turned to Dad. "I tell you, I know how to get across! I can do it! I'll shows those Ruskies! There's hundreds of 'em out there, maybe thousands, with rifles and machine guns," he said slurring his words. "They think they got the border all closed down, but they don't! They're as dumb as cows standin' in the rain waitin' for someone to lead 'em in. Ain't one of 'em know this area. I tell you, I can get across! They can't stop me!" He pounded a fist on his chest with pride.

Father shook his head and glanced at Mrs. Geiger. She looked alarmed. The man was very drunk, his eyes bloodshot and half closed.

132

"You stupid, ungrateful people. Here I be risking my life for a bunch of strangers, and you just sit like idiot pigs waitin' for slaughter! Well, I'll show you!" He pointed a threatening finger at us and left.

I stared at the spot where the old farmer had stood just seconds ago. *He seemed so sure of himself. Yes, he was drunk, but he said he knew where the border wasn't closed down and, escaping at night would be excellent cover for us. Imre took us during the middle of the day when everybody could see us! We should have gone with him. The worst that could happen to us would be to get caught again. So what? There were so many prisoners at the barracks this afternoon, and most of them were released.* I looked toward Dad, ready to argue my point.

Dr. Geiger was saying something about Sándor, the man who'd nearly scared me to death when he appeared suddenly out of the darkness near the train station. We were to go with him in the morning to another village. It was closer to the border, and Sandor had relatives there who could help us.

"All right, little ones, let's get you to bed," Mrs. Geiger's soft voice said. Mom took Anikó and Andorina by the hand as Mrs. Geiger led the way upstairs.

"Dad..." I began seeing my opportunity, "...I think we should have gone..."

Father interrupted me before I could finish my sentence, "András, I'm very tired, and I'm sure Dr. Geiger is too. We have to talk about how we might get across tomorrow, so please, if you're going to sit with us, just listen, okay?"

I nodded my head, feeling defeated. Hardly listening to what Dad and Dr. Geiger were saying, I fixed my eyes in the direction of the front door.

An hour later the drunk farmer stormed into the house again, holding an Austrian flag high above his head. "I told you!" he said triumphantly.

Mom and Dad stared in amazement. Dr. Geiger's eyes grew wide and Mrs. Geiger shook her head, "How did you...?"

"I told you I could gets across! Here's the proof!" he interrupted her, shaking the Austrian flag in his fist. He threw the flag on the floor and walked out.

My heart was pounding! We could have gone across! He knew! If we'd gone with him, we would be free by now! I looked at Dad. His face was grim. Mrs. Geiger's shoulders sagged.

"He's going to tell everyone tomorrow."

"So what are we going to do?" I exclaimed, angry and upset. "We should have gone with him! We've been sitting around doing nothing!

Dad jerked his hand up to hit me.

"Kálmán, don't!" Mother said, alarmed.

"We weren't going with that drunk!" Dad said, trembling with anger. His face was flushed and damp.

I swallowed hard, barely nodding, afraid to move or breathe.

"Kálmán," Mom broke in. As he turned to her, I released a rush of air from my lungs. "Why don't we get some sleep. We can talk more about this in the morning."

My mind went blank. I didn't care anymore. We could have escaped, but Dad had decided not to go with the old farmer. He didn't care what I had to say.

I slid out of the chair and followed Mrs. Geiger, Mom and Dad upstairs. Reaching the attic room, Mother looked at me standing in the doorway. She walked over, lifted my chin with her hand, and looked into my eyes. Without a word, she gently pulled off my sweater, shoes, socks and pants and led me to a cot in the corner of the room. Covering me with the large comforter, she sat and held my hand.

"András, you were very brave this afternoon at the barracks. Without your help, we would never have gotten away from that horrible place. You've been a big help and very courageous. I love you very much." She kissed my cheek.

Early the next morning, before sunrise, as we waited for Sándor, I stood looking out of the living room window. Everything was black, the sky, the rotting wood of the barn, the bare trees. I wondered if we were ever going to get out of this country. I struggled to remember what day it was: Tuesday, November 27th. Counting on my fingers, I realized with surprise that we'd left Budapest on the 22nd! *We'd been trying to escape for six days! And Andrea and the Olivérs got across four days ago!* I stared at my fingers. Six days of trying. I could no longer imagine that we'd make it safely across the border. We'd been shot at, captured and imprisoned. We had failed miserably. We couldn't do it. Everyone kept saying that the Russians were sending thousands of more troops into the small villages along the border, strengthening their patrols, shutting down every avenue of escape except, of course, the one that the

135

drunken farmer knew, but Dad would never agree to let him take us. It was impossible. We might as well go back to Budapest. I resigned myself to never seeing Andrea again and sent a silent prayer, wishing her luck and happiness in her freedom.

Mom, Dad and Dr. Geiger were sitting behind me making plans for our escape that I knew wouldn't work.

Father nervously said, "We can't continue going from village to village along the border without being caught. I don't know why the secret police didn't take our identification papers when they arrested us, but they're useless without the proper stamp for the zone near the border. Regardless of which village we're in, if we're stopped by soldiers or the police, the first thing they'll ask for are the ID papers. If we could get the mandatory stamp on the papers indicating we can officially stay in this zone, it will give us the time we need to come up with a plan."

"But the only way you can legally get your papers stamped by the authorites is to prove that you've got a job within the zone." Dr. Geiger replied.

"We'll have to go to the city of Sopron. I know a few builders and contractors there. If I can find them, they might be able to sign me up for a construction job and give me the needed papers so I can register with the local police. Once I have that stamp, we'll be able to stay in the area for a little while anyway, without being arrested."

"But how will you avoid the guards on the train? They're approaching everyone who gets on and off the trains and demanding to see their papers."

"I don't know," Dad shrugged.

"There's one other problem," Dr. Geiger continued. "János has probably boasted to several people about crossing the border last night and talked about your refusing to go with him. It might be dangerous for you to board the train here in Lövő." He paused briefly. "I'll ask Sándor to take you to a small village just north of here. You can board the train to Sopron there."

Mother's worried eyes darted from face to face.

We had to make it to Sopron without getting caught!

CHAPTER SIXTEEN

LOST FROM THE FAMILY

Sándor pulled up in front of the house with a horse drawn cart. Quickly pulling on our coats, we hurried to the door. Mom turned to Dr. and Mrs. Geiger, "We'll always remember your generosity and kindness." She hugged them tenderly.

High cheekbones and a friendly, lopsided grin greeted us as we climbed into the cart and headed toward the train station. Father sat up front with him. Mom, the twins and I rocked in the back of the old cart under a canvas blanket Sándor had provided for us. The horse climbed slowly up the side of a hill. It's nostrils flaring, steam rose from them as he struggled with the weight of the cart. The trees were bare and the grass yellowed and browned by winter.

A constant, gentle rain splattered my face, penetrating my worn clothes. Tired, cold and wet, I felt miserable. The twins were asleep under the blanket. There was nothing to see except my breath forming gray clouds against the dark morning sky.

"Pretty little city, Sopron. Do you know anyone there?" Sándor asked casually after riding in silence for some time.

"No. We're just going to get our papers stamped," replied Dad.

Sándor nodded. "Where are you going afterwards?"

Dad tensed, hunching his shoulders, the muscles in his jaw jumping nervously.

Sándor stole a glance at him then turned his attention back to the road. "It's a shame to go all the way to Sopron and not see some of the sights. The architecture, especially the churches, is well worth seeing. There's a nice little church just a few blocks from the train station...to the southeast on Deák Square. You might want to drop in there."

I thought Mother was asleep. She'd closed her eyes soon after we'd left Dr. Geiger's. Suddenly her eyes flew open as Sándor finished his sentence. "Is there a name?" she asked.

Sándor grinned and tugged on his cap. "I'm afraid I don't have a name, but I've heard the church has been very helpful to city folk."

Dad nodded his understanding and whispered "Thank you."

His brown cap pulled low over his head, Sándor didn't say more as he drove the creaky cart along narrow, rutted country lanes, avoiding the more comfortable, paved main road.

It took close to an hour to get to the train station, which turned out to be a simple shed with a door but no windows. It was in the middle of nowhere, surrounded by fields.

Dad bent down toward the twins, huddled against Mother's legs. "Listen carefully. Once we go inside, I don't want you saying a word. Not a sound. Understand?" He turned to look up at my half-closed eyes. The lecture was unnecessary. My brain wasn't functioning, and my body was screaming for sleep.

We entered the dank shed slowly. A single dull light bulb hanging from a wire created ugly shadows. A wooden bench ran along three walls of the shed. Adjusting my eyes, I saw that the shed was full of people, farmers from the surrounding villages. This had to be the only train station for miles. There was nowhere to sit down so we stood, clustered together, facing the door. I could hear the slow, rhythmic breathing of the strangers, the rustling of packages as they shifted their bundles for better comfort. Slowly, I let my eyes move across their faces. Some were old, weather beaten, with hard lines running from eyes to mouth. Others were fairly young, tired and drawn. As my eyes roamed their faces, I realized most of them were staring at us with curiosity and something else. I turned my eyes toward the door quickly. *What was it? There was something in their faces...something... They knew.* My body stiffened with fright. *That's it, they knew!* I felt hot beads of sweat break out on my forehead. *They knew why we were there! They knew we were trying to escape!* A wave of terror washed over me. My hands bunched into tight fists. *Every one of these strangers knew the only reason city people would be standing in this old shed was to get to the border.* I prayed none of them was a spy.

The train finally arrived, and we hurried on, taking a seat in the back of a car, not daring to look at or speak with anyone. I closed my eyes as soon as we sat down, locking out the world, building an invisible shell around myself to contain my growing fear.

I felt the train slow down for what seemed like the hundredth time.

Dad shook me hard, "András, wake up!"

I rubbed my eyes and looked out of the window. The train was pulling into the city of Sopron. For some reason, soldiers had not entered the train during its many stops. Each small station we'd pulled into had a few guards who merely peered into the windows, but none of them came on board. And although a conductor passed through our car twice, he never asked for tickets from anyone!

"András," Mom called urgently, "we can't be stopped and questioned once we get off the train. We have to avoid that at all costs." She pointed toward my left, "Since everyone's getting off at the platform leading to the station lobby, we're going to go to the right. As soon as the train stops, I want you to swing that door open and start walking. Dad and I will get the twins."

Nodding rapidly, I pulled on my coat and cap and moved to the crowded area by the doors. Everyone was facing the left door. Pushing my way back toward the right, I firmly grabbed the cold handle of the other door. Mom, Dad and the twins were stuck in a mass of people surging toward the exit. I felt the final lurch of the train as it stopped. The door by the platform was opened immediately and a stream of people pushed their way down the steps of the car. I craned my neck, looking for Mom and Dad behind the surging crowd. The instant I caught sight of them, I jerked the other door open, jumped down and froze. Directly in front of me, across the tracks, stood five soldiers, their rifles casually slung over their shoulders. They were staring at our train. They were staring at me! I turned to rush back into the car and collided with Dad, holding Anikó in his arms.

I jerked my head in the direction of the soldiers. Dad saw them and quickly turned, pushing Mother and Andorina back into the car and out the open door by the platform.

"Come on!" he whispered. "We have to get into the crowd!" He set Anikó down and turned to Mom, "Put her down!" he pointed at Andorina. "They're searching for families. They'll have a hard time seeing the girls among all of the legs and packages."

We hurried to catch up with the mass of people streaming toward the lobby. I dug my hands into my legs, grabbing my pants tightly to force myself from breaking into a run. Walking rapidly next to Mother, I looked down and reached for Andorina's free hand, squeezing it gently. She gave me a curious smile. Mom let go of Andorina, indicating to me to fall back into the crowd. It would be less obvious that we were one family.

Entering the lobby, I dared myself to look around. A handful of soldiers and policeman stood silently, scanning the crowd. Taking a deep breath, I focused my eyes on the strangers legs in front of me and concentrated—left, right, left, right, left, right. Andorina toddled along silently. When we reached the steps leading from the building, I slowed down and looked up for Mom and Dad. *They weren't there! How could I have lost them? We couldn't have been more than six feet behind them!* Stopping, I stood up on my toes, frantically searching the crowd that poured into the square. A big man bumped into Andorina, almost knocking her over. He said something harshly and pushed past us. Grabbing her by both arms, I moved quickly to the safety of a tall, square column, part of the entrance to the train station. I pushed Andorina against it and desperately looked around. The square was wide and filled

142

with people. My eyes darted along the street to the left, then quickly scanned the area across the square. People were hastily walking out of the dull, gray box-like apartment buildings. Others were entering the small grocery store, and the cafe next to it was doing brisk business. I stared down the broad street directly across from the train station, straining to see a familiar face. I couldn't find Mom and Dad anywhere! My throat hurt terribly. I tried to swallow the rising panic that clutched my throat like a powerful hand. I could barely breathe. *Where were they?*

"Excuse me, are you lost?"

I whipped my head around and stared directly into the face of a young soldier. I stepped back quickly, smashing into the column, knocking the air out of my lungs.

"Uhhh,...we...." I couldn't think of what to say!

"Well, no need to panic. Come on, I'll take you to the police substation. It's just a few blocks from here." He reached out to lift Andorina into his arms. I grabbed her, pulling her up to me. The soldier looked at me suspiciously.

"I...we're waiting...for Mother," I finally managed.

"Well, where is she?" he asked slyly.

"She...uh...went to buy something."

The soldier's clear gray eyes searched my face. "Well, you two young kids shouldn't be standing here alone. Someone might bother you. I'll just stay here until your mother returns. By the way, where are you from?"

The blood drained from my face. We had to get away from him! If Mom or Dad showed up, he'd ask for the identification papers! I knew I had to say something fast.

143

Breathing deeply, I summoned all of my courage and smiled at the soldier.

"That's very kind of you sir, but you don't have to stay with us. We'll be fine. I can take care of my sister. I do it all the time!"

"That's good, little comrade."

I flinched as the soldier patted me on the head.

"Where'd you say you were from?" His voice was more insistent.

"Oh, we're from a nearby village," I responded confidently, my mind frantically searching for a way out.

"And which village would that be?" His voice was hard and cold.

Hugging Andorina to me, I glanced into his impatient face, then at the street. "Hey, there's my Mom. Thanks for watching out for us! Bye!"

I ran into the square and started down the street, Andorina bouncing in my arms. I glimpsed back at the soldier quickly. He was shouting something and walking rapidly in my direction. I ran hard, dodging people on the sidewalk, bumping into briefcases and packages. As I jumped off the sidewalk a strong arm grabbed the collar of my coat. I felt the wind knocked out of me as I was slammed against the wall of an apartment building. A large, stocky man, with powerful arms and legs looked at me through dark, angry eyes. The soldier appeared suddenly and glared at us.

"I told you how many times! Why do you disobey me! I ought to whip you right now! Look at the trouble you've caused this good soldier!" The large man looked up into the soldier's grey eyes.

"If this boy of mine has caused you any trouble, I apologize."

The soldier glared at me. "You said you were waiting for your Mother!"

The large man spoke immediately, "Oh, he's always playing practical jokes. He's a terrible liar. Why, I've had to go see the principal at his school three times this year!" He shrugged his shoulders.

"Well, you'd better teach him a lesson!" The young soldier shook an angry finger in my face. "Go on! On your way!" he shouted harshly and turned toward the station.

I looked up at the large man.

"It's okay now, little brother. I saw the soldier bothering you. When you ran away from him, I thought I might be able to help."

I nodded, still frightened and unable to speak.

"Now, where are your parents?"

"I...I don't know." I stammered.

"Well, where were you going?" His concerned eyes and gentle smile eased my panic.

"To the church...somewhere near the train station."

"Oh," he nodded knowingly. "Well then, it's not far from here. Come."

He reached out his strong hands and effortlessly lifted Andorina to him. I hurried along, his powerful legs moving

145

in long strides. We reached the church, just six blocks from the train station. As the stranger rang the doorbell to the minister's house which was attached to the church, he looked down at me.

"Our country needs young men like you, but perhaps your parents have the right idea. If you stayed, you'd grow up always being afraid. And as a man, you'd be angry and bitter." He sighed and shook his head. Tears filled his sad eyes. "Little brother, when you get across the border and breath the sweet air of freedom, think of me."

A woman with light-brown hair and a warm smile answered the door. "Oh, there you are! Thank goodness!"

The large man set Andorina down gently and turned to leave. I called after him. "Sir! Thank you for helping my sister and me."

His kind, dark eyes twinkled. With a quick nod and a wink, he hurried away.

"András!" Mother cried as she rushed to the door. Anikó was right behind her and upon seeing Andorina, she took her twin sister by the hand and led her inside.

"Where's Dad?" I asked as Mom pulled my wet coat and cap off.

"He's out looking for you."

"Oh," was all I could manage.

Mom introduced me to Éva, the minister's wife. Her smile was radiant, and her voice friendly and warm. Éva took me into the kitchen, treating me like the most important person in the house. She made hot chocolate and buttered my bread as I told her, Gábor the minister, and Mom what had happened to Andorina and me. I spoke in short, slow sentences. My entire body ached for sleep.

"Mom?" I started my question as soon as I'd finished my story, "Do you think Dad will come back soon?"

"Yes..." Mother began, looking somewhat lost. "Before he left he said he'd come back here every hour just in case you showed up."

"Good," I mumbled.

"Your father will be back soon, András," Éva said reassuringly. She stood and pulled on my arm gently. "Come on, you're falling asleep at the table. You too, girls. Hop down and follow your big brother. I have two nice, warm beds with lots of soft blankets."

I smiled as she led the three of us up the winding stairs. Helping the twins with their sweaters and pants, Éva chatted brightly about the wonderful lunch she was going to make. Her movements were fluid and calm. The twins looked like rag-dolls in her hands, totally trusting her actions, her words. She tucked the twins in, nuzzling them as if they were her own children. Turning to me, Éva bent and kissed my cheek. "Sleep well," she whispered. Looking at her soft, kind face, her light-brown hair pinned into a loose bun, I felt relaxed and sheltered. The run-in with the soldier faded into a distant memory. It seemed so very long ago since I'd felt absolutely safe, protected from soldiers and police, from the freezing embrace of winter, from my own fears and doubts. Here in the soft, warm bed with Éva's smile lingering in front of my eyes, I willed all of my memories to melt away, focusing only on the comfort and warmth of this place.

As I started drifting off to sleep, Mother quietly entered the room, looked at the twins and gently sat down on my bed.

"I wanted to tell you before you fell asleep...we're escaping today!"

"Today?" I blurted as my body bolted upright in bed.

"Yes. The minister has friends who can help us. Now, go to sleep, and we'll tell you about it when you get up." Mother kissed my forehead and left.

I felt the excitement of hope fill my body. But my mind kept pulling me back, cautioning me, reminding me. *We tried before and failed. The bullets that screamed around us as we ran were meant to kill us. They wouldn't hesitate to shoot at us again, and someone could be killed.* I fought the images rising in my mind's-eye but was helpless to stop the terrifying pictures. Dad, a bullet exploding in his chest; his look of surprise. Mom, shot in the back, falling to her knees, crying out for the twins. I screamed silently, begging the images to disappear. I wanted so much to believe we were going to make it this time! We had to!

CHAPTER SEVENTEEN

OUR LAST HOPE

Mother's voice woke me shortly after 1:00 p.m. She was coaxing the twins awake, telling them what a fine lunch Éva had waiting for us downstairs. I sat up quickly and dressed. The promise of a good, hot meal made my empty stomach grumble with anticipation.

Dad and the minister were already seated at the table as we entered the kitchen.

"Good to see you, son," Dad said quietly as I gave him a hug.

He ruffled my hair affectionately and pulled out the chair next to him. "Your Mother told me what happened. I'm proud of you."

I sat down with a grin, struggling to keep the nightmare images from returning. Éva served a wonderful meal throughout which she expressed her joy and pleasure at having such a fine family at her table.

After lunch, Gábor and Mom helped Éva clear the dishes. I took the twins by the hand and followed Dad into the small, warmly furnished living room.

"Dad," I began before he sat down, "Mother said we're escaping today." I raised my eyebrows.

Father sat comfortably on the couch and tugged at his mustache. "Yes. Gábor made some phone calls while you were asleep. A friend of his named Zoltán will come to take us across."

My mind exploded with questions. I looked at Dad and tensed, seeing the doubt in his eyes. "What about the stamp we need on our papers? Did you get that?"

"No. Gábor said it would be too dangerous. We were very lucky when I was interrogated at the barracks that they didn't check to see if I'd been in prison. According to Gábor, they'd ask the same question at the police station here, and well, they could arrest me for no reason and then check my background."

I couldn't believe it! "No stamp?" I asked, feeling my anger soar. "Where is this Zoltán going to take us across? The border's heavily guarded!"

"I know, but we must try! This may be our last chance, our only chance!"

"Maybe we should go back to Budapest" I mumbled.

Father leaned forward, resting his elbows on his knees, staring at the floor. "We have to try."

"Why?" I almost shouted. "We've lost Andrea and Grandpa, and Imre's in jail!"

Looking up sharply, Father froze me with his gaze. "We're doing this for you...all four of you. You're too young to really understand, András and they," he said, pointing to the twins, "have no idea. You'll understand all of this when you're older. You have to trust that your mother and I are doing what's best for you."

I didn't understand and felt defeated and frustrated by his explanation. Quickly standing, I took three short steps, then spun around and faced him. "Didn't the minister tell you anything else about how we're going to escape?" I demanded.

"No."

"Did he say who this Zoltán is?"

"No."

"How can the minister be so sure we'll get across?"
Dad sighed. "He isn't. Look, we have to trust him.
That's all. There's no one else who can help us." He stood
and walked out of the room.

Dad returned to the living room a short time later with
the minister. They sat facing each other.

"Zoltán will be here at 3:00. He's a young man, single."
The minister spoke calmly to Father.

"Where do you think he'll take us across, Gábor?" Dad
asked, an edge of anxiety in his voice.

"I'm not sure, Kálmán. I haven't asked him, and I don't
want to know. The less I know, the less I can tell the
police or Russian soldiers if they should ask me." Gábor
smiled at Dad, continuing easily, "Zoltán has relatives in
the tiny village of Harka, right by the border. Just across
the border is the Austrian village of Deutschkreutz. Perhaps
that's where he'll take you. His relatives should know the
patrol schedule of the border guards."

Dad smiled weakly. He looked extremely tired and
worried. I forced myself to look at the calm, relaxed body
of the minister, willing myself to feel the same way. I knew
once Zoltán arrived, the anxiety and fear of the past seven
days would surge through me like a rollercoaster out of
control.

The doorbell rang at exactly three o'clock. Zoltán smiled as we were introduced to him. "Well, a fleeing family of five!"

We quickly said 'goodbye' to Gábor and his wife. I hesitated as Éva released me from her warm hug. I think she knew I didn't want to leave.

Zoltán had a bicycle, and he promptly picked Anikó up and sat her on it. Looking at Andorina's questioning face, he smiled at her. "Unfortunately, my poor bicycle has only one seat. But of course, you'll get to ride too!"

Tall and lanky, Zoltán's thread-bare wool pants clung to him. He wore his gray cap pushed far back on his black hair. The cold, drizzling rain hit his face softly. We walked through the city quickly, Zoltán cautiously taking us along the eastern edge of town, down the narrow, less travelled streets to a country road which led south. In silence we passed meadows and plowed fields, scraggly bushes and tall, bare trees. Zoltán gave the twins turns sitting on his bike as he pushed it along. They both looked tired, but neither of them said a word.

An hour later, we came upon a small village. As we walked along the narrow road lined with old, single-story houses, three farmers carrying shovels and hoes came toward us. When they reached us, one of the farmers, without looking in our direction, casually commented, "Be careful. The Russians are over there." He pointed to our left with the shovel and kept walking. I spun around, staring at the three men, once again realizing how obvious it was to the locals that we were from the city. They knew we were headed toward the border just by looking at us. We were totally exposed! I felt the sudden nausea of panic slam into my body. I looked up at Mom and Dad, hoping to be reassured, but both of their faces were grim and determined. When we rounded a bend in the road, I saw a small hill to the left, a short distance away. Three Russian tanks and a group of soldiers waited at the foot of the hill, all facing our direction.

Zoltán's back stiffened and his knuckles turned white as he gripped the handlebars of the bicycle. He glanced briefly in the direction of the tanks without slowing down. I pulled my cap lower over my forehead, keeping my eyes on the tanks. A few of the soldiers stared at us as they climbed onto the huge machines. I forced myself to look at the road in front of us. We couldn't escape them! My eyes searched the fields frantically for some sort of shelter, somewhere to run to, away from the huge guns on the tanks. There was nowhere to hide from them! I trembled uncontrollably, waiting for the awful rumbling sound of the tanks to follow us. I glanced back quickly as we continued our steady pace along the road. The tanks sat there like three gray elephants, their trunks stretched toward us. They weren't moving! I wanted to shout with joy as the distance between us grew.

It was getting dark as we entered another small village. Zoltán turned to Father. "This is Harka. Just a little farther to my relatives' house." He looked at his watch and turned toward me with a smile. "Well, it's 4:45 p.m. I hope you enjoyed our pleasant little stroll through the country. We mustn't do this again."

I grinned at him with a tired smile, suddenly realizing we had been walking for almost two hours!

We hurried along the main street past squat houses and turned toward the plowed fields at the outskirts of the village. Reaching a short street with buildings only on one side, we quickly walked to the very last house.

Zoltán introduced us to his aunt and uncle. They obviously weren't expecting us, nor were they happy to see five strangers invade their small home. Nevertheless, they treated us well, offering bread, butter, and tea while we waited. The uncle told us matter-of-factly that the entire area was patrolled around the clock by border guards.

Zoltán left to check the footpath alongside the fields. He knew exactly where the guards walked, he just wasn't certain what time they were scheduled to pass by.

Zoltán hurried through the front door thirty minutes later, "Now!" he ordered.

We quickly tugged on our wet coats. Mom took the scarfs Anikó and Andorina wore around their necks and pulled them up over their mouths. "From now on, don't say a word. Okay?" The girls, their eyes wide, nodded obediently.

Dad looked at me. "András, absolutely not a word once we step out the door!"

I nodded, pulling my scarf over my mouth not to keep from talking but to keep the icy cold air from searing my throat.

Hurriedly saying goodbye to Zoltán's aunt and uncle, we stepped out into the damp December night. Each twin was flanked by two people, Anikó between Mom and Dad, Andorina between Zoltán and me.

We walked along a narrow, muddy road. My feet sank into the cold muck, covering my ankles and seeping into my shoes. Andorina had to lift her knees high to pull her small feet out of the ooze. Walking as quietly as possible, I peered through the darkness. The fields were plowed under for the winter. Between the large, bare fields, rows of tall, looming trees stood like soldiers at attention. In the distance, dotting the landscape, small forests stretched far into the cold night. I wondered how in the world Zoltán, or anybody for that matter, knew exactly where the border was. Before the rebellion at the end of October, wide rolls of barbed wire stretched along the entire border, creating a deadly barrier. Tall, wooden guard towers stood 150 yards apart. These clearly marked the border between Hungary and Austria. Zoltán's uncle told us the farmers in the villages along the border had removed the barbed wire and dismantled most of the guard towers. So how could anyone know when they crossed the border? There weren't any signs, not even a pile of rocks. Nothing, just empty fields.

Zoltán stopped and turned toward Dad. "See those large lights in the distance?" he whispered.

I craned my neck and saw the small, bright spots far away.

"That's the Austrian village of Deutschkreutz. The Austrians have been very helpful to us. They've erected tall poles with huge lights on top so we can see exactly where the border is. Once you reach those lights, you're on Austrian soil."

Dad nodded quickly, his warm breath mingling with the cold night.

Zoltán immediately continued walking. He led us along the muddy road another five minutes then turned onto a small foot path that ran between the plowed fields. Large bundles of corn stalks lay like dead logs in the fields. Looking up toward the lights, toward Deutschkreutz, my heart soared with hope.

We walked maybe twenty yards on the narrow foot path when Zoltán suddenly stopped and faced Dad again. "This is as far as I go," he whispered urgently. "Look over there, toward the lights. Can you see that tree to the right of the lights?"

Father concentrated in the direction Zoltán was pointing. I squinted hard, trying to find the outline of the tree. It was pitch black except for the bright lights in the distance.

"To avoid the guards and their dogs, go along this path as far as the tree. At the tree, turn directly toward the lights. When you reach a small creek, turn to your left and keep going until you reach the country road. That road will lead you into Deutschkreutz."

Father clasped Zoltán's hand warmly. "Thank you, my friend."

"Good luck." Zoltán replied and turned to retrace his steps along the foot path leading to the muddy road.

We immediately started toward the tall, bare tree. I tried to gauge the distance between us and the tree. Seventy, maybe eighty or even one hundred yards. The total darkness surrounding us made it difficult to accurately estimate the distance. My wet feet had long-since gone numb as we plodded along the path. Andorina and I walked in front of Mom, Dad and Anikó. I kept my eyes on the towering lights in the distance. This was going to be easy, like spotting a church steeple in a small town. All we had to do was walk toward it and eventually we'd reach our goal.

I turned instantly as I heard Dad whisper something. I was about to ask him to repeat what he said when I heard voices behind us. I froze in terror. It wasn't Father I had heard whispering! People were talking harshly somewhere behind us on the path or perhaps the road. I strained to hear what was being said, but the voices seemed far away. *It had to be the border guards! They must have caught Zoltán!* I screamed at myself to move, run toward the lights!

"Lie down! Now!" Dad hissed and yanked me down onto the cold, wet foot path. I fell face-first into the mud, flattening myself against it, trying to sink deeper like a frog concealing itself from its prey. Mother protected Anikó with her body, Dad, Andorina. I saw him look at the corn stalks. We could still hear the arguing voices behind us. I tried to determine how far away they were and cried silently for Zoltán. *First Imre, now him. We were bad luck to everyone who tried to help us escape.*

"Come on!" Dad whispered and grabbed Andorina. He rushed into the field, past three bundles of corn stalks and frantically pushed Mom to the ground, the twins on top of her. I threw myself to the ground next to Mom. Dad sprawled on top, cross-wise to protect us. I desperately hoped we looked like the corn bundles from a distance. Mom's breathing was short and hard. The twins, sandwiched between her and Dad, looked terrified. I felt sorry for them, realizing they had no idea what was happening. Like little puppets, we had yanked them from one place to the next. Their lives during the past six days

157

had been filled with strangers and fear. And here they were, cold, wet, their coats caked with mud, not knowing why they were lying in a plowed field instead of at home in their warm cribs.

I strained my ears in the direction of the voices. My entire body was numb from the mud and freezing cold air. The voices began dying away. I waited for a signal from Dad. It seemed like hours had passed. Finally, Dad pushed himself up, grabbed the twins and set them on their feet. Mom and I sprang up, mud plastered on our coats, heads and legs. Silently, we stole back to the foot path and headed toward the tree. I shivered, as much from fear as from the cold. Reaching the tree, Dad turned directly toward the large lights and stepped from the path to the plowed field. I stared at the bright lights in the distance, willing them to be closer. It was impossible to estimate how far away they were. The only sound was our labored breathing and our feet slapping against the cold mud.

Shots suddenly exploded around us! A split-second later, a bright red flare burst into the dark sky! I panicked, feeling the rush of a scream burning in my throat like a fireball! Dad's strong hand jammed me in the back, forcing me to the ground instantly. He fell hard next to me, pulling Anikó under him. Mother was cradling Andorina. I jerked my head up at the bright, red sky. The flare slowly curved downward. My hands grasped at clumps of dirt as more shots whistled past us. I didn't want to be caught again! I trembled with a fear I'd never known before. It exploded in my brain and slammed against my forehead like a sledgehammer. And then it occurred to me that being captured was the best thing that could happen. But I knew it was a distant hope. They didn't want to catch us, they wanted to kill us!

The rifle shots were coming from our left. As soon as the flare died out, Dad jumped up, "Hurry!" he whispered harshly and sprinted into the dark. Gasping for air, we reached the small creek where Zoltán had told us to turn left.

"We can't go left! That's where they're shooting from!" Dad looked about frantically. "Come on!" He took off, running with Anikó like a ragdoll in his arms. I leaped after him, my heart pounding wildly.

Another flare burst into the sky. We threw ourselves to the ground. In the light of the flare, I saw a long row of thick bushes 200 to 300 feet away. I grabbed Dad's arm and pointed at them. If we could reach the bushes, we'd be well hidden from the flares. Shots rang out loudly around us! With a sickening feeling rising in my throat, I realized the bullets were coming from the direction of the bushes. It was the way Zoltán had told us to go!

The instant the flare fell to the fields, we jumped up and ran in the opposite direction of the bushes, quickly reaching the edge of another creek. It was narrow and shallow, but the banks were very steep and slippery. Dad jumped into the freezing water and lifted each of us across. We continued running toward our only hope, the towers of lights. I began to sweat with panic. The darkness was disorienting. It was impossible to gauge how far we were from the border.

More flares lit up the black sky. Each time, we threw ourselves hard to the ground, not daring to breathe or move until the flare had died. Between flares, we ran hard, backs bent, eyes staring at the lights that might save us.

We came to another creek. Dad slid in, the icy water reaching above his knees. One by one, he carried us to the other bank and scampered out after us. We ran straight, the row of bushes now far behind to our left. I slipped on the steep banks of the next creek and gasped for air as the shock of the icy water hit me. Dad jumped in and grabbed the back of my coat, lifting me with his strong arms. He quickly pushed me up the opposite bank. I shivered uncontrollably as he waded in the waist deep water carrying the twins and Mom across. Quietly, he told us, "We might reach the country road if we turn left here."

Taking Anikó's hand, he headed toward the lights. I clamped my mouth shut tightly to keep my teeth from rattling. My wet, cold clothes clung to me like icicles. Walking fast, I looked down at Andorina hurrying beside me, her short legs struggling to keep up. I was amazed she and Anikó hadn't started crying yet.

I looked toward the lights again. They seemed so far away, and I suddenly felt totally exhausted. I could barely lift my feet. Forcing my stinging eyes away from the lights, I silently begged Dad to stop. We were lost. I was lost. I was freezing to death. My muscles ached with each step and my brain was paralyzed with fear. I wanted this to end! There was no sense in it. We should stop now! We could sit down and wait, either for the soldiers or for daylight. It didn't matter to me. I just wanted to stop! I wasn't in control of my legs anymore. They weren't listening to my silent screams. I followed my parents blindly, tripping over rocks and frozen clumps of dirt.

CHAPTER EIGHTEEN

ON AUSTRIAN SOIL

Dad climbed up a small incline and stopped. I struggled to pull Andorina up with me. The surface was flat. I looked down at my shoes. I was standing on a paved road! I jerked my head toward Dad. He was smiling at Mother.

"It's the country road! We made it!" Mom said with disbelief.

I felt disoriented and confused.

"We're in Austria!" Dad shouted with joy.

"In Austria," I mumbled, dumbstruck as if the wind had been knocked out of me. It dawned on me slowly, like staring at a hidden picture puzzle and suddenly seeing the picture.

Dad leaned down toward the twins, "Okay kids, you can talk now."

Anikó grabbed Mom's hand, yanking it hard, "Let's never go back!"

Andorina pulled the scarf from her face and began crying quietly. Still dazed, I stooped down and hugged her. She wrapped her short arms tightly around my neck. Her hot tears of relief brought me back to reality. "It's okay! You can cry as loudly as you want to! We've escaped!"

Exhausted and stunned by our success, the five of us held hands and walked briskly down the road. I saw a shadow of a figure coming toward us. As we neared, he gestured for us to stop. It was an Austrian policeman. "Halt," he yelled harshly. We didn't stop. We didn't even slow down. Mom and Dad grinned with delight as we marched right up to him.

Dad spoke in German, "We're so happy to see you!" The policeman eyed us for a moment, then smiled.

"Stay on this road. As you enter the village you'll see a school building on your left. Go there."

"We'll go wherever you tell us to!" Mom responded cheerfully leaning toward the policeman. I thought she was going to kiss him!

We marched into the village as if walking on air. The few people we passed stared at our mud caked clothes and faces. We entered the school lobby, which consisted of two rooms, the door between them standing open. Several women, scarfs on their heads and laced boots on their feet, sat next to a blazing wood stove on one side. A tall, very thin elderly man with a nicely trimmed white beard stood in the center of the room. He wore green leather knee britches with thick socks and a matching jacket. There was an air of elegance about him which surprised me.

Reaching out his hand to Father, he said, "Welcome to Deutschkreutz, Austria!"

Dad shook his hand warmly.

"Please, step this way," the gentleman indicated the adjacent room with a sweep of his hand. Stepping into the warm room, I was shocked to see it was full of Hungarians. The Austrian pointed toward the bathrooms where we hurriedly washed the mud from our hands and faces. We went back to the room full of refugees and were immediately served hot, sweet tea and buttered bread. As I gazed around the room, tired faces turned toward us knowingly.

162

"Dad," I said urgently, "did all of these people escape?"

Sipping the hot tea gratefully, Father looked around. "Yes, just like us."

"But there's got to be forty or fifty people here!"

"That seems right," he answered nodding his head.

"But how did they all get out?"

"I guess the same way we did."

"But, didn't anybody get shot?"

Dad's face tensed instantly. "That's a stupid question! Be quiet and eat your bread!"

I flinched at his harsh words and quickly stuffed bread into my mouth.

"Kálmán, please, don't be angry now. We're in Austria." Mother quietly pleaded.

Father's shoulders sagged slightly. "Austria or not, it was a stupid question," he replied softly.

As we finished eating, two plump women came and escorted us into what I guessed was the gym in the school. The floor was covered with straw mattresses, many of them already occupied by sleeping refugees. The two women pointed at a group of empty mattresses, then turned to Dad and me. "You can't go to sleep wearing wet clothes. Come." Mom nodded and headed to the mattresses with the twins.

Dad and I followed the women down a short hallway. They took us into a dimly lit classroom and indicated several boxes filled with clothes. As soon as they shut the door, Dad and I stripped off our soaked shirts and pants, quickly pulling on dry, warm garments. When we stepped

163

out of the room, Dad turned to me. "I'm going back to the lobby for a while. You go ahead and get some sleep."

"I'm not sleepy!" I replied cheerfully although I was extremely tired. I wasn't ready to end the day. I needed more time to let our escape sink into my brain.

"Okay, come on."

It was ten o'clock. We stood in the lobby with a few Austrian women and men, and Dad asked them if they remembered a family named Olivér, with three children, coming through here on November 24th. I looked into their faces one by one, desperately hoping that in four days they hadn't forgotten the name or the way Andrea looked when she walked into this lobby. The Austrians searched their memories, shrugged and told us that so many people had come through, it was difficult to say for certain if the Olivérs had been here. They told Dad that the refugees only stayed the night. They were moved to other villages each day to make room for the Hungarians escaping the following night. Father thanked them and stepped over to speak quietly with others who had crossed the border this evening. I wasn't listening as more and more Hungarians kept arriving at the school. I watched them come in, some smiling happily, others grim and scared. I became increasingly upset as people kept coming into the lobby. *It was our night! Our success! We should be the only ones who had escaped, who'd been shot at, who'd made it across the freezing, muddy fields!* I sat down next to the stove, feeling angry and insignificant.

The warmth from the stove seeped into my tired body. I closed my eyes for a moment, focusing on the comforting heat.

"Where's the nearest telephone!" an arrogant voice demanded.

Jolting upright, I rubbed my eyes.

"I said I need a telephone!"

I looked at the stranger standing in the center of the lobby. He was middle-aged and extremely well dressed. His long, warm coat was magnificently tailored and expensive. He wore a soft, fur cap, and a silk scarf around his neck. He was holding a briefcase.

"The only telephone is in the Post Office building," a young Austrian responded, looking at the man curiously.

"Where's the Post Office!"

"It's 12:30 a.m. The Post Office is closed. You can make your call in the morning."

"I can't wait until morning! I have to call Vienna now! Wake up the Post Master!"

I kept my eyes on the elegantly dressed man. I couldn't believe what he was demanding. I saw Dad standing quietly near the door, facing the stranger.

"You have to wake up the Post Master! Do it now!"

Everyone in the lobby was staring at him. The stranger looked at their faces in disgust. He reached toward the collar of his coat and turned it up. I was stunned. Sewn into the underside of his collar were a sparkling diamond bracelet and necklace. Father suddenly reached out and grabbed the man's silk scarf, yanking him hard. The expression on Dad's face was a mixture of embarrassment and anger. In a low, forceful tone he addressed the stranger.

"Who do you think you are making demands on these good people? You remind me of the filthy secret police! Take your worthless diamonds and rude behavior and go back the way you came! Now apologize to them! If you don't treat them with the respect they deserve, I'll drag you back across the border myself!"

The tall man stared angrily at Dad, opened his mouth to speak, then closed it without saying a word. He yanked his coat collar down and stormed into the adjacent room.

Father looked at me, "Come on, let's get some sleep."

I stood and followed him slowly into the dark gym. Slipping my shoes off I quickly collapsed on the straw mattress, wondering what was going to happen to us. We were safe now but without anything—no home, no money, nothing except the clothes on our backs. And, we were without Andrea.

CHAPTER NINETEEN

THE SEARCH FOR ANDREA

It was nine o'clock when I opened my eyes and scanned the room. Nothing registered in my sleepy brain. I couldn't remember where I was. I saw mattresses all over the floor, some with sleeping strangers, most of them empty. I turned to see the twins lying side-by-side, facing each other with eyes open and their thumbs in their mouths. I shook my head to try and clear it. Mother sat up, smoothed back her hair and smiled at me.

"Come on András, help me with the twins."

I slipped my muddy shoes on and helped Andorina with hers. Dad woke and rubbed his face. He smiled at the twins. "Good morning my brave refugees!"

An Austrian woman came toward us with a bright smile. She handed us towels, a shoe brush and two rags. We washed up in the school bathroom, then went outside to brush and wipe as much of the dry, caked mud off of our shoes and coats as we could.

At breakfast, the tall, thin old Austrian who had greeted us the night before approached our table with a knowing smile. "Perhaps you would like to take a little stroll and get some fresh Austrian air when you've finished your meal."

"That would be wonderful," Mother replied cheerfully.

"What's going to happen to us?" I asked quickly.

"Well, young man, now that you are free, perhaps you can decide what should happen."

His reply surprised me. *How could I decide!* Dad laughed.

"This is the first time I've seen you speechless, András!"

"You and your family will be taken to another village shortly after noon," the old gentleman addressed Father. "We need to make room for those who'll be escaping tonight."

We finished breakfast and stepped out into the street. I turned in the direction we had come from the night before, looking hard into the distance. The two-lane, paved road looked like any other country road. Bushes and trees were clustered intermittently on both sides, and beyond lay the fields. My eyes frantically searched the road, desperate to find the exact spot where we first stepped on it, the exact spot where we knew we had made it across. But it all looked so ordinary, not at all different from the country roads in Hungary. It was a bitter disappointment to me. It took us six terrifying days to escape, and now I couldn't even find the spot where we had first set foot on free soil! I turned and followed my parents.

As we reached the slight curve in the street just past the school, Mother suddenly stopped. "Look Kálmán, there's a green car! And look there, there's a yellow truck!" she exclaimed in astonishment.

I stared at her for a moment before realizing what she was saying, then I shouted with joy. "Colors!"

Mother smiled at me brightly. "Yes, András, colors! You remembered!"

We walked on, calling out the many colors we saw. The homes along the main street of the village were one- and

168

two-story dwellings, white-washed with thatched roofs. An old woman was leaning out of the window of one of the homes, looking at us as we approached along the sidewalk. When we reached her, she leaned toward the twins and handed them bright red apples.

"Here, little ones, take them." The kind smile on her old, lined face was so sweet! The twins took the apples hesitantly, then looked up at Mom.

"It's okay, go ahead and eat them." Mother said, then looked at the old woman, "Thank you, thank you very much."

We strolled back toward the school slowly, people passing us on the street nodding kindly. I was amazed at how happy Mom and Dad looked! The joy in their faces was so unfamiliar to me! If this is what freedom did to them, it was wonderful!

We reached the school and entered the gym just in time to hear a young Austrian man announce that those Hungarians with children should follow him. We went outside and saw a large truck with several families already seated on the flat-bed.

"Where are we going?" I asked the man helping us onto the truck.

"North to the town of Eisenstadt," he replied cheerfully, lifting the twins onto the truck.

There were twenty-five people on the truck, fifteen of them children. Some of the men and women smiled at us and told us how they had escaped. Others, their eyes still filled with fear, didn't speak at all.

The night before in the school lobby, I overheard some refugees talk about how the Communists were sending spies into Austria to find Hungarians wanted by the government. Their goal was to force people back to Hungary, especially the scientists, engineers, architects and doctors. They were desperately needed. The rest, the nonprofessionals, the blue collar workers, would be put on trial. That was why no one on the truck mentioned their last names and why Mom and Dad spoke very little to the strangers around us.

We rode for hours through the peaceful countryside, past villages and fields, thick forests and the mountainsides where the Austrians grew their grapes. The sky was gray with threatening black rain clouds.

The truck stopped in front of a large military base in the city of Eisenstadt. I noticed that none of the Austrian soldiers who helped us off the truck had guns. We were ushered into a building with a huge, open room. Two long tables with soldiers stood to one side. We were told that everyone who escaped from Hungary was brought to this processing center to be registered. We stood in line, awaiting our turn. The soldiers at the tables spoke with each family, registering names, date of escape, and previous residence. When our turn came, Mom and Dad anxiously asked about the Olivér family, hoping the Austrians had a record of their arrival. They looked through their papers carefully. The name Olivér was not registered. Andrea and the family had not come through Eisenstadt. Mom looked around helplessly as we stood up. I was confused. *It didn't make sense! If all of the Hungarians who had escaped into Austria were registered here, they had to have some record of Andrea!* I suddenly realized with a sickening feeling that the only reason they wouldn't be registered here was because they hadn't made it across the border! But Imre told us they escaped! My mind went numb. *All this time I believed Andrea was safe in Austria!*

After registering everyone, we were escorted back to the truck and travelled north, toward the Austrian capital of Vienna. It was several hours before we arrived at the small, well-kept village of Velm. The truck stopped in front of a large, U-shaped house. Stretching back from the house, on either side, were stables and a barn, a large dirt yard between them. Everyone wearily climbed down from the back of the truck to spend the night. My family was escorted to a small room in the house. It had three beds and a stove in one corner. A young girl brought us a tray of food, smiling shyly as she told us the bathroom was down the hall. The twins looked expectantly at the tall stack of freshly sliced bread, cold cuts, white cheese and hard boiled eggs. Their wide eyes twinkled eagerly. Mother smiled at them. "Okay, girls, let's eat!"

The twins rushed to the tray, piling mounds of food on their plates.

"Dad," I turned toward Father sitting on the bed across from me. "What are we going to do? What's going to happen to us now?"

Father sighed and shrugged his shoulders. "I don't know exactly. All the owner of this house knows is that we're to spend the night and then move on. He didn't know where they'd take us next."

"Somebody has to know! Can't we just leave, go somewhere on our own?" I said with frustration.

"Kálmán," Mom interrupted excitedly, "why don't we go to Vienna? My mother's family still has relatives there.

171

I told you about my Aunt Zsan. And my friend Gretel lives in the city. Of course, I haven't been able to visit them for eleven years, but I did write them occasionally. I'm sure they would help us."

Dad ran his hand through his dark brown hair. "Well, we can't just shuttle around from village to village. Everybody's been very kind, but I don't want to rely on them to take care of us."

I sprang from the bed excitedly. "If we go to Vienna, maybe we can find Andrea! I mean, it's the capital of Austria, right? Maybe we can talk to some officials or go to....I don't know, wherever there are refugees like us and ask about the Olivérs!"

Mom lowered her head as her eyes filled with tears. Dad sat without moving, then quietly said, "We don't even know if they made it across the border." He sighed and closed his eyes. "But both of you are right. We should go to Vienna. I'll talk to the owner of the house in the morning. He may know someone in the village who's driving up there." Dad opened his eyes and looked at Mother. "Write down as much of the addresses that you can remember for Aunt Zsan and Gretel. I'll find them."

Dad found a ride to Vienna early the next morning. Restless and bored, Mom insisted I take a long walk with her and the twins. When we got back to the house, I saw some of the other Hungarian kids playing soccer in the courtyard and immediately joined them. I focused all of my attention on the game. Running and shouting, we played until we were totally exhausted then slumped against the barn, breathing hard, our faces red. I felt incredibly happy. I hadn't thought about Mom or Dad or Andrea or our escape.

Going back to our room, I plopped on the bed and fell into a deep sleep. A knock on the door woke me late in the afternoon. Mother opened the door to a tall stranger, his hat in his hand.

"Hello. You must be Justine Máday. I'm Robert, your Aunt Zsan's nephew. I'm here to take you to Vienna."

Mother stared at him without speaking.

"Your husband Kálmán stayed in Vienna with Aunt Zsan. He sent me to get you. I have a car out front."

I sprang up from the bed. "Come on, Mom. Let's go!"

Mother looked lost for a moment, then smiled at Robert. She turned anxiously to the twins. "Okay everybody, get your coats on!"

We arrived at Aunt Zsan's apartment in Vienna less than an hour later. When she opened the door, I saw the grandest lady ever. She had to be at least 70 years old! Her floor-length dress was a beautiful deep blue, and her white hair was piled high on her head in a loose bun. She leaned gently on a cane with a silver handle, but her back was straight, and she held her head high. Her speech was very proper, but her voice was soft and kind. When we sat down, she turned to Mother. "I know what you need—a warm bath."

Mother's face lit up. None of us had had a proper bath for a week!

Dad came to the door smiling, "I've already had mine."

After all of us had bathed and eaten, Aunt Zsan apologized that she couldn't put us up for the night in her small apartment and explained that she had reserved a room in a nearby hotel. Soon after Robert dropped us off at the hotel, Mom called her friend, Gretel. They had met during summer camp when they were kids and had remained close friends through all these years.

Gretel showed up at the hotel with three large bars of delicious chocolate! Anikó, Andorina and I sat on the big bed eating our chocolate silently. Gretel stared as we stuffed the chocolate into our mouths.

"Justine, they're going to get sick. You can't let them eat the whole bar!"

Mom looked at us, chocolate smeared on our hands and mouths. "It doesn't matter, Gretel. I won't take it away from them. I won't take any food away from them. They've known hunger for too long." I smiled at Mom and silently vowed that I wouldn't get sick from eating the chocolate, that I wouldn't ever get sick from eating.

Gretel came to the hotel the following day at noon and told us she had found a place where we could live until we decided what we were going to do. She drove us to a small community called Purkesdorf, just outside of Vienna's city limits. We stopped at a large government-run clinic and retirement village. Three buildings had been designated for refugee families.

It was a wonderful place. The entire area looked like a park with lots of trees, bushes and gardens between each structure. Our building had 20 rooms, all occupied by Hungarians. We were given one room which had a large bed and two smaller, single beds. At the foot of the large bed stood a wooden table with chairs. A small sink stood near the door. We shared the bathroom facilities with the others on our floor. The main window of our room faced the street. Across the street was a gas station and a small cafe. The other window faced toward the center of the clinic area, providing us with a beautiful view of the landscape. Every day, someone from the clinic cafeteria brought us our meals. The Austrian refugee relief organization gave us money for general expenses like soap, toothpaste and clothes.

Mother enrolled me in the local school and tutored me in German every evening. There were other Hungarian kids in the school, and we quickly formed a soccer team. Dad immediately began working in Vienna with the American division of ICEM, the refugee relief organization. His job was to interview Hungarians who wanted to live in the United States. Through ICEM officials and the Hungarians he met while working there, Dad started an intense search for Andrea and the Olivér family.

On November 24th, the day Andrea and the Olivérs left with Imre to cross the border, Mother gave them the name and address of a family friend in Vienna. He was the Assistant Minister of Education in Austria. They agreed that, if we somehow lost each other after escaping, each family would contact the Assistant Minister. He was to be our touchstone. Unfortunately, when Mom went to visit him, all he could tell her about the Olivérs was that the Red Cross had called him late in November and told him that the Olivér family had successfully escaped. They didn't give him any information about where the family was.

Mom and I took the twins to Vienna often. I loved going to the city! The large, wide streets were filled with

175

cars and the sidewalks crowded with people. Shops everywhere displayed their brightly colored goods and the delicious smells from the bakeries and candy stores always made my mouth water. We frequently visited Gretel and Aunt Zsan, both of whom always had a treat for the twins and me. Aunt Zsan and her nephew also came often to Purkersdorf, always with packages of clothes and food. Gretel brought bananas and grapefruit on one of her visits. The twins didn't know what to do with the fruit. They had never seen a banana or grapefruit before!

Soon after arriving in Purkersdorf, Mom wrote to her brother Béla in California to let him know we had escaped but that Andrea had been lost. She told him we would stay in Austria until we found her and that Dad had decided the family would settle in New Zealand.

It was late in January of 1957 before Mom received a long letter from Uncle Béla. She let me read it and showed it to Dad that evening. I knew Father had his heart set on moving to New Zealand, and that Mother dreamed of going to the United States.

In his letter, Uncle Béla said there was only one country we should live in, and that was America. He wrote amazing things about his life in California, most of which I couldn't believe or even imagine. When Dad finished the letter, he sighed and looked at Mom. "I guess we're going to California."

Mother jumped up and hugged and kissed him. Her dream was coming true!

The next day, Dad went to the U.S. Embassy in Vienna and registered our family for sponsorship. But we couldn't go anywhere until we found Andrea.

Dad searched desperately for information about her and the Olivér family at every refugee organization in the city. He sent letters to all of the countries in Europe which had accepted Hungarian refugees.

Near the end of February, Dad came home early one day incredibly excited and happy. Father explained in a rush of joy that a fellow inmate from the prison in Budapest, named Attila, walked into the ICEM offices that morning. When Father told Attila that he was searching for Andrea, Attila smiled broadly and told him he knew where she was. Attila said he met Andrea a few days ago in a refugee camp in Lucca, Italy. He had recognized her from the picture Father had kept of Andrea while in prison! Attila said he introduced himself and asked Andrea if she was Kálmán Máday's daughter.

I couldn't believe it! During the past twelve weeks, I had struggled silently with the terrible feeling of certainty that I'd never see my older sister again. All of my hopes and fears about finding Andrea had died. I pushed thoughts of her out of my mind. It was the only way I could deal with her loss. I felt confused as Dad talked about her excitedly. The voice in my head that had convinced me to accept I'd never see Andrea again fought against the thrill and relief I felt at finding her.

The next day Dad went to the Red Cross and filled out the necessary papers to bring Andrea back to Austria. In early March he took a train to the Italian border and met Andrea and the Olivér family. When Dad brought her to Purkesdorf late that evening, Anikó ran into her arms. I had a thousand questions to ask her, but Andrea was withdrawn and quiet. It wasn't until a week later, as we were walking alone in the park, that Andrea told me how

177

scared she'd been. When we didn't show up the day after she'd escaped with the Olivér family, Andrea said she thought we'd been captured or killed. She assumed she'd never see us again and had accepted the Olivér's offer of adoption. It was going to take time, she told me, to get used to being with her family. I never told her that I had given up hope of ever seeing her again.

Within a week of her arrival, the U.S. Embassy in Austria approved our going to America. We were the 30,000th refugee family they had accepted. Mother was beside herself with joy, repeating for us the few English words she knew.

We landed at a military base called Camp Kilmer in New Jersey on March 23rd, 1957. As we flew low over New York, Mom excitedly pointed out the Statue of Liberty, explaining it was the most important symbol of what America stood for—freedom. I really didn't know what she meant until shortly after landing. A soldier escorted us to lunch. When I stepped into the large dining room, my jaw dropped! Right in front of me was a long, wide counter filled with more food than I had ever seen before in my life! The soldier gave us trays and plates and indicated that we could eat anything we wanted and as much as we wanted! I stared at him and the counter full of food! I filled my plate quickly and walked back to the soldier. Holding my overflowing plate out toward him, I joyously said, "Freedom!"

In addition to the wonderful amounts of food, clothes, books and unlimited opportunities to bathe, the base showed movies every night. It was the first time I'd seen a film! I told Mom and Dad I wanted to stay at the base forever!

We stayed for three wonderful weeks. All of us had to go through days of physical examinations and tests, and Mom and Dad spent a lot of time being questioned by different officials.

They explained to the officials that we wanted to settle in California. There were several organizations, companies and churches which had registered as potential sponsors for refugees. It took some time for the officials to find a sponsor that could accept a family of six.

On April 6th, we left Camp Kilmer and flew to California. A church in Pomona had volunteered to take us in. The minister, his wife and a man named Mr. Brickbauer, who spoke German with Mom and Dad, met us at the airport. They drove us to a single-story house. Mr. Brickbauer explained that a member of the congregation owned it, and we could live there free as long as we wanted to. The house was fully furnished and in one of the bedrooms, the bed was piled high with clothes, linen and towels. Mr. Brickbauer asked us to sort through the clothes in the next few days. He'd pick up what we couldn't use and take it back to the church.

Dad approached the huge pile of clothes and began pulling out various pieces, telling Mr. Brickbauer we didn't need them. The minister and his wife looked confused. They couldn't understand how Dad knew we didn't need the clothes without us trying them on. Mom turned, saw their questioning looks and in English, said, "Red. Communists' red. Red star. Red flag. No red in this house!"

CHAPTER TWENTY

RED ROSES

"You really don't have anything red in your house?" asked Jennifer amazed.

"No. No red." András replied matter-of-factly.

Jenny stared hard at him. "How come you never told anyone about your escape? It's incredible. Does Coach Edwards know?"

András shrugged. "No. I don't talk about it."

"Well you ought to!" Jennifer leaned forward. "Brad and Mike and the others wouldn't laugh at your accent if you told them."

"Brad and Mike don't care...wouldn't listen." András replied heatedly.

"Well, you didn't think I'd care!" Jennifer retorted. "Are you ashamed about it?"

András jumped to his feet. "No!"

"Well, how's anybody supposed to get to know you if you don't talk about it?" Jennifer stood quickly. "Brad can be an idiot, but if you explained why soccer's so important to you and about your escape..."

András interrupted her. "No!" He grabbed his gym bag and flung it over his shoulder. "I'm quitting. I'll tell Coach Edwards tomorrow after the game. I don't want to play with them any more."

He stepped directly in front of Jenny.

"You're the best player they have. Everyone knows that. You can't quit!"

András tried to step around her. Jennifer didn't move.

"Are all Hungarians as hard-headed as you are?" she asked loudly and let him pass.

András climbed down the ladder quickly, grabbed his bike and looked up at the treehouse. Jennifer stood at the top of the ladder, her hands on her hips. He felt a sudden sense of regret at leaving her mad.

"Thank you for...just thanks." András jumped on his bike and slowly peddled toward home.

The game was against the Wildcats, a powerful team with excellent players. András stood on the sidelines as Coach Edwards called out the starting line-up. He knew this was his last game with the team, and yet he felt the wonderful rush of excitement as he trotted onto the field to face his opponents. It was going to be a challenging game, very fast and rough. The whistle blew. András watched the ball sail high into the air. Mike and an opponent jumped after it, their necks craning, arms spread wide. Mike's tall body propelled him higher. The ball crashed against his head and flew toward his teammates.

Minutes before half-time the game was still scoreless. András was soaked with sweat, his teammates tired and sore. Running hard after the ball, András hooked it with his left foot, spun quickly away from the Wildcat defender and turned toward the sideline. Concentrating on keeping the ball inbounds and under control, he raced toward the goal.

"Go András! Go András! Goal! Goal!"

András jerked his head toward the team bench. Jennifer was standing at the front of a large group leading the cheer. András stared. They were the kids from his sixth grade class! He couldn't believe it. And right next to them was Elizabeth, Jennifer's older sister, with a group of her friends each waving a pompon. *When did they arrive?* he wondered.

His heart pounding wildly, András nearly tripped over the ball! Quickly turning his attention back to the game, he looked up to see a Wildcat almost upon him. Spinning right, he kept the ball close to his feet. The defender reached his side, throwing his long leg out toward the ball. András spun again and saw two more defenders coming toward him. He broke into a sprint. It wasn't the best strategy but the roar of the crowd excited and challenged him.

Rushing toward the net, the goalie made the mistake András had hoped for—he ran out to meet the ball instead of waiting for it to come to him. András pumped his arms hard, looked left and kicked the ball to the right with one swift move. *Goal!* He stopped instantly and bent forward, breathing hard. The crowd cheered wildly. It was half-time.

András trotted toward the sideline. Brad, Mike and the rest of his teammates watched in shocked surprise as the crowd surrounded András, slapping him on the back and shaking his hand.

"My sisters never come to the games!" Brad remarked in amazement.

"Looks like they found a reason," Mike replied still looking toward András and the crowd. "That was an excellent play," he stated, turning toward Brad.

"Yeah. So, he's expected to make goals." Brad replied sarcastically.

"So are you. So am I. But we haven't even gotten near the goal the entire first half," said Mike.

"Maybe it's the accent. Girls think guys with accents are mysterious," Ed, the goalie, chimed in.

Brad threw a towel at Ed. "That's the stupidest thing..."

Mike interrupted, "Whatever it is, András is a fantastic player."

Brad stared at Mike then turned his gaze toward the crowd. "Yeah, he's good...real good."

Mike stood up and started toward András.

"Hey, where ya going?" Brad called.

"To congratulate him." Mike replied. Ed and several other players joined Mike.

"You've gotta be kidding." Brad remarked.

"What's not to congratulate? He scored a beautiful goal and he's surrounded by girls!" Ed replied as the group walked toward András.

"We're a team." Mike added over his shoulder.

Standing next to Jennifer, András draped a towel around his neck.

"So when are you going to tell Coach Edwards that you're quitting?" Jennifer challenged.

András took a sip from his water bottle and shrugged. "Maybe I'll just..." He faced Jenny, a slight smile forming at the corners of his mouth. "How did you get so many kids to come to the game?"

"They wanted to come. I didn't twist any arms, I just talked with my friends. They wanted to see you play. Do you know why they've never come to a game before?"

András shook his head.

"Because no one invited them! I've heard kids talk about you and the team at school, but they didn't know how to approach you. They think you won't talk to them because you're embarrassed about your accent. Now that's silly!"

"My accent?" András asked.

"Elizabeth thinks it's cute, well that's not the exact word she used but..." she stopped suddenly.

Both of them stared in the same direction. Mike and the rest of the team were walking their way.

"They better not do anything..." András began, his fingers curling into tight fists.

"So what are you going to do, quit?" Jenny asked pointedly.

András spun his head around, anger blazing in his eyes. "Stop asking me...." András shot a glance at the crowd around him. They were here to watch him play. He looked back toward his approaching teammates. "No, I'm not quitting." András said with determination as he faced Jenny again. "I'm going to become better...the best soccer player in the city."

184

Jennifer smiled broadly and gave András a quick hug. Stunned by her closeness, he turned away quickly and came face to face with Mike. András set his jaw.

"Hey, I just wanted to...that is, we just wanted to congratulate you for the goal. It was a great play." Mike said extending his hand to András.

"Thank...thank you." András stumbled over his words. He kept his eyes on Mike as his teammates shook his hand.

"It's the accent, right? I mean, you're a refugee. You couldn't afford to pay all these kids to show up." Ed ran his sentences together as he gazed at András. "Maybe it's your nick-name, Attila-the-Hun, it sounds so...so strong, so manly! Listen little Attila, think of a good Hungarian nick-name for me will ya? Something that will keep the other team from scoring."

András stared at Ed for a moment, unsure if he was being serious until he saw the hint of a smile in Ed's eyes. Ed let out a loud laugh. Mike shook his head and joined the laughter. András smiled and breathed deeply. He wasn't sure if he'd ever understand American humor. Right now, he knew it didn't really matter. They had finally accepted him as part of the team. He stole a glance at Jennifer. She had reached out to him, questioned him, supported him. He would thank her again, after the game. Perhaps send flowers. Red roses were a possibility.

The End